Southern Dreams

Hidden

Dreams

I0737627

BOOKS BY DIANN SHADDOX

A Faded Cottage

Whispering Fog

Miranda

Spirits of Sacred Mountain

The Gatekeeper

Hidden
Dreams

DIANN SHADDOX

Hidden Dreams

By Diann Shaddox

ISBN -13-978-0-9976111-8-2
ISBN -13: 978-0-9976111-9-9
ISBN -13: 978-1-7371331-0-0

This is a work of fiction. All characters, places, businesses, and incidents are from the author's imagination. Any resemblance to actual places, people, or events is purely coincidental. Any trademarks mentioned herein are not authorized by the trademark owners and do not in any way mean the work is sponsored by or associated with the trademark owners. Any trademarks used are specifically in a descriptive capacity.

The unauthorized reproduction or distribution of this work is illegal. Criminal copyright infringement is investigated by the FBI and is punishable by up to 5 years in federal prison and a fine of $250,000.

ALL RIGHTS RESERVED:

No part of this book may be reproduced, stored in a retrieval system, or transmitted, in any form or by any means, without the prior permission in writing of the publisher, nor be otherwise circulated in any form of binding or cover other than that in which it is published and without a similar condition including this condition being imposed on the subsequent purchaser. You do not have resell or distribution rights without the prior written permission of both the publisher and copyright owner of this book. This book cannot be copied in any format, sold, or otherwise transferred from your computer to another through upload, or for a fee.

Eagle Quill Publishing
www.eaglequillpublishing.com
First print Edition May 2021
Printed in the United States of American
Hidden Dreams Copyright © 2021, Diann Shaddox

*This book is dedicated with love to Randy, my husband,
and to all my friends I grew up with.*

Acknowledgment

To Marsha Tolleson Rhodes, my editor:

Thank you for your encouragement, kindness, your patience, and the many hours you have spent working with me. I will be forever grateful for everything you've done.

To Hidden Dreams Cover Art:

Crossways, circa 1815, Aiken, SC. Crossways originally served as the main home for an antebellum plantation. Crossways is rich in history, style, and symmetry with generously proportioned rooms and restored architectural details. Over 200 years old now, Crossways represents the grace, ease, and elegance of a time past.

Hidden Dreams

Prologue

This is my life, not what I had planned, nor my dream, but nonetheless – my life. I am a young woman with many chances to marry, but ultimately all for convenience, a loveless and passionless marriage. Many people in these parts call me a beautiful woman with my long red hair flowing down my back and round green eyes. However, my calling card for all of the young men in the county is my home Bella Oak, the largest plantation with over eight hundred acres, in Spring Hill, South Carolina.

This night is the same as most of my nights. Nothing has changed. Not true, my dreams did change. The wonderful hidden dreams of a young girl have become twisted and turned going down an altered path. Not a path I'd chosen if destiny hadn't set in, but my path anyway. Now I sit, just as I've done my entire life in the old, white wicker swing that is worn from years of use, on the massive veranda of Bella Oak Plantation.

Ole Betsy, my daddy's old hound dog, moves slowly in a circle and then she lies near the top step of the porch guarding the aged plantation home. The dog yawns with a small howl and breaks the silence of the night. The swing moves with ease by a gentle push from my feet as it glides back and forth. I listen to the katydids serenade in the night as they blend in harmony with the croaking of the recently hatched tiny tree frogs. The warm moist air of the spring day is becoming cool. It is telling me that this day is finally ending.

The peaceful night becomes dark. However, I'm able to make out the silhouette of a man standing in front of me. I want to reach out to him and touch his sweet caring face. I hesitate. I feel every muscle in my body aching. I look down at my callus, blistered hands as I draw them back behind me. I am a true mess, sure not a southern belle that everyone presumes by any means. I try to control my emotions. I grip my hands tight and let my nails bite into my flesh to control my emotions. The young man standing in front of me grins with a mischievous that shows in his bright blue eyes. He winks, telling me my life will be all right. I feel a stabbing in my chest and the pain intensifies.

The young man reaches out his hand to me and I gently put my tired, rough hand in his. For a fleeting second, I feel his tender touch and then – he is gone. My body did feel the love, the passion that I'd missed. A sensation stirs inside of me just as it did in a time long ago wanting to surrender itself.

My tired eyes close and I soak in the stillness of the night. However, I'm now alone listening to the familiar creaking of the old chain of the swing that is hanging from the veranda ceiling. I caress my leather journal to my chest. The one I started when I was a young girl. I've memorized the words that my journal contains. I read my memories keeping them alive of a tender sweet love story of my hidden dreams. I draw in in a deep breath and I begin to read the words, the tales of my southern dreams….

•••

CHAPTER 1

Bellamead Planation July 3, 1960

The day was sweltering. It was Sunday afternoon and a time that blended hundreds of years of the past with the present. The Spanish moss draping in the knotted live oaks that surround the old plantation home for centuries softly sway in a gentle breeze. The paddle fans swish in a steady rhythm overhead on the wide verandah as they serenaded the red haired, young girl. Her young fingers brushed the wild hair from her face revealing her dark green eyes.

From the outside looking in this was a perfect life showing a true southern belle that was sitting on a verandah of the largest plantation home in the county. All that was missing was her huge flowing dress and her entourage of beaus riding up on their magnificent steeds, each wanting to win her hand in marriage, along with the plantation.

Charlie Bellamead, her name everyone used except her mom and Pearl who used Charlene, wasn't a southern belle at all. She was a true southern girl full of mischief. She knew there were many beaus ready to win her hand and many of them would be here for this Fourth of July picnic. The best and largest picnic around the county since 1844, only missing its picnic during the Civil War not even the Depression interfered with the celebration.

Charlie wiggled her shoulders. Her hands laid flat behind her on the smooth pine floor. She pulled in a deep breath of the fresh summer air that was full of a hint of pine needles along with the sweetness of blooms from the gardenia bushes lining the front edge of the verandah.

The long chain from the swing creaked loudly. It startled her making her eyes squeeze tight. She suddenly shoved her secret hidden thoughts back into her mind. Her long bushy ponytail swung with the motion of her head and landed on her moist back. Her long legs crossed Indian style as her eyes peered up.

Martha, Charlie's mom, sat in the white wicker swing that was hanging on one end of the large verandah. The woman's speckled gray hair lay on top of her head in a tight knot. "It's mighty hot today," Martha said as little sweat beads grew on her forehead. She waved her colorful fruit printed apron in the air gently fanning herself. "I hope we get a good thunderstorm this afternoon, one that's full of rain," added Martha in a slow southern drawl. "I reckon this heat ain't letting up." Her eyes stared up at the cloudless blue sky. Her head shook no.

This summer had already broken a record for the hottest June for Spring Hill, South Carolina. One hundred degree weather had begun the first of June right after school was out and hadn't let up. The only rain had been a small drizzle a few weeks ago not even enough to wet the ground. Charlie saw the worry grow on her mom's face making deep wrinkles form across her mom's brow. She knew the truth that when you own a plantation, hot dry summers sure ain't what you wish for and this summer heat wasn't letting up.

"Mom, can I go swim at Rock Creek?" asked Charlie, inhaling a deep breath of warm humid air.

Charlie while she waited for her mom's answer threw the small red ball onto the porch floor letting it bounced. She made one sweep and all the jacks were swooshed into Charlie's hand. She smiled. Her nose scrunched making the freckles across her nose wiggle. Charlie was the jacks champion around these parts and no one was able to beat her.

Her mom wasn't paying attention to Charlie. She leaned back in the old swing finally relaxing. She began humming to the song that was playing on the radio sitting next to the window in the living room.

"Honey," questioned Martha bringing her thoughts back, "did you see Myrtle Mae at church this morning?" The woman leaned over while the swing slowly glided back and forth with ease from the gentle push of her feet. She picked up the oversized dented dishpan full of unshelled black eye peas that was sitting on the porch floor and became busy shelling the peas.

"Yes," said Charlie nodding her head. "I talked to Myrtle Mae at church this morning."

"I declare that girl should've stayed in school another year," Martha said with a slight moan shaking her head from side to side. Her barefoot feet pushed the floor making the swing's chain crackle disturbing the quiet afternoon. "But her and Bobby Joe ran off and got married yesterday."

"That was her dream, marrying Bobby Joe, but she should've waited until she finished high school. Except – I don't think she could." Charlie ducked her head not letting her eyes meet her mom's questioning eyes.

Martha sat quiet for a few seconds pondering her thought. She didn't comment on Myrtle Mae's condition, since that'd be a topic for all the women to gossip about at the picnic tomorrow, especially with Miss Ethel, a busy body from town.

"I heard they're going to blend Tanner and Stonebridge plantations," Martha quickly added. "Something you and Jeffery could do, blend Bella Oak and the Montgomery plantation."

"Dang it mom." Charlie's eyes jerked up. She sat quietly watching for her mom's response. "Stop – pushing me to marry Jeffery." She muttered in a soft whisper, "I despise Jeffery Montgomery."

"Now honey don't get so riled up, but it shore would help out your daddy," she paused, "if you married him – having a son in law like Jeffery. That boy would be able to handle a large old plantation like this. Most of the boys around these parts wouldn't even know how to start taking care of her." Her head swung back and forth. "This old plantation is just too big."

"I'm not gonna marry him or anyone for a long, long time," Charlie added taking in a sharp breath. "I'm going to leave and travel the world."

"You and that dream of yours… Charlene, Jeffery's very wealthy and not bad looking and many girls around here would jump at a chance to marry him."

"Good – let 'em. I've got plenty of time to get married." Charlie moaned with her temper flaring causing her face to become red. Her eyes squinted as she dreamed of her life living away from this old plantation.

"We'll see. Jeffery is graduating this year," her mom continued. The woman's face tightened with those watchful eyes peering down at Charlie. "He'll want to settle down soon and he'd be happy to plan a wedding right after your graduation next year, when you turn eighteen." Martha's thumb slid down the peas as she shelled them with years' experience, letting the black-eyed peas trickle into the dishpan.

Charlie scrunched her face. Things were always the same. Her mom never wavered, everyday adamant she was going to marry Jeffery Montgomery. Living in this old plantation and even in the small town of Spring Hill, nothing ever changed. People were born, lived here their entire lives, then died and the next generation did the same, year after year. But not her, she was breaking free and leaving this small town. She was going to see the world.

"Well, these peas ain't going to cook on their own," Martha said.

The swing jerked to a stop. She slipped her shoes on and the swing crackled when she rose cradling the dishpan full of shelled peas in her arms.

"Now Charlene, you don't get into that spring creek without someone there with you," she added shaking off the pea's hulls on the floor that were clinging to her apron.

"I won't Mom, I promise," answered Charlie, stretching her long thin legs out in front of her.

"I mean it," Martha declared with a snap of her fingers. She became quite for a second and gave Charlie a stern look. "Joshua said he's killed a few ole moccasins down at the creek and there might be more. He'll go back down to the spring with ole Betsy tomorrow to see to 'em."

"I'll be careful Mom, I promise."

Martha's body tensed. She didn't move. She stood there looking down at Charlie still sitting on the porch floor. "Now, honey, I don't want to frighten you, but there shor' is more than snakes that might be hanging around down at that creek, more of a two legged kind. That ole scalawag Hudson has been spotted down there. Your daddy has seen him a few times near the shed by the smokehouse. Your daddy doesn't mind sharing food, but he shor' won't put up with stealing, and we've been missing some meat that he butchered last fall."

Martha took in a deep breath. "You and Ramona need to be careful. I don't like that man's intentions, especially toward young girls. He is just plain ole trash." She gradually turned her body back to the screen door.

Charlie squeezed the jacks tighter in her hand, piercing her palm. Her heated eyes moved over to the small table between the rockers. She stared at her peashooter, the name her daddy had given her small pistol that laid on top of the table between the rockers.

"Don't worry mom, we'll be fine," she called back.

"This heat! Lor' ha mercy, it shor' ain't helping the crops this year," Martha mumbled. She wiped her brow with the back of her hand stepping into the house, softly closing the wooden screen door behind her.

Hurriedly, Charlie leaped down the large steps and off the verandah. She quickly felt the heat her mom was talking about as sweat began to build on her neck. Her head moved back and forth swishing her ponytail, freeing her hair from her clammy neck. Her fingers touched her peashooter that was strapped on her hip.

Charlie raced down the hill to the curvy path, even though it was hard to breathe in the smothering air. When she heard the loud roar of the large green tractors, she stopped by the edge of the woods and tried to catch her breath. Her eyes swung to the fields that were behind the old plantation home. She could see dust flying as the tractors followed each other. She was worried along with her mom about her daddy and Joshua. She understood that this old plantation was becoming too hard on her daddy, Everett, giving her a guilty feeling about Jeffery and now of her dreams of moving away.

She looked back up the hill at the old plantation home. It was standing tall surrounded by its soaring pines and Cyprus trees showing its character and its own personality, similar to Charlie with a strong perseverance that nothing was going to get the better of either one.

CHAPTER 2

Rock Creek

Charlie darted along the path toward the spring fed creek that was known as Rock Creek. The creek flowed to the side of the old plantation home, the most precious water source for years for the Bellamead family. She entered into the thick forest of trees their branches entwined from hundreds of year's growth letting her hide from the sun's heat. Her fiery pace halted. Her mind drifted off as she stepped back into time. A calmness came over her as she soaked up the coolness in the air letting the wetness on her face and neck quickly disappear.

The cool breeze blew above her as it rustled in the tree limbs. Overhead the cardinals and mockingbirds sang, in addition to the mournful cooing of the doves trying to call for rain. This was Ramona Ledford and Charlie's magical world.

"Finally," came a soft voice in the quietness of the afternoon. The girl's blue eyes peered up at the bouncing red headed girl coming at her. "I wondered if you were going to be able to get away," the young girl sitting on the bank of the creek called out.

"Sorry Ramona," Charlie answered, "I had to help my mom pick some peas when we got home from church."

Charlie sat down on the cool grass and quickly untied her new white tennis shoes. She slipped them off and laid them on the bank of the

creek. She stood. Her long legs reached over and carefully she placed her foot onto a slick, round rock as she made her way across the creek's new bridge; the one that she and Ramona had built out of rocks a few months ago.

Charlie stood on the rocks for a few seconds letting the water in a steady stream flow over her feet. Her body shuddered.

"Wow!" she shouted. "Burr, the waters cold." She didn't move as she studied the huge rocks the two girls had placed precisely to dam up the flow of water from the spring to make a perfect swimming hole. Charlie laughed. "The missing rock in our dam looks like a big smile with a tooth missing," she added as she stepped near Ramona and sat down. "Have you been here long?"

"Nope," Ramona said leaning back on her elbows letting her long blonde hair blow in the soft breeze. "After lunch I had to help Momma for a while."

Charlie lay back against the cool earth on the grassy bank staring up into the tall trees. "Alright, this is…nice."

"Yep, it's so cool down here," answered Ramona.

"Oh…" Charlie sat up. "I almost forgot, my mom said we need to be careful. Joshua has killed a few snakes down here, and he'll bring ole Betsy to see if he can get some more. Daddy doesn't want any problems with snakes for the Fourth of July picnic."

"Yes," squealed Ramona, enthusiastically sitting up! "The fourth is almost here. Is everyone coming to the picnic?" She asked turning her head from Charlie trying to hide her reddening face as she blushed.

Charlie stared. "I think so, it's the same group as always and yes, you don't have to worry." She sucked in a deep breath. "Jeffery is going to be here too, unfortunately." Charlie puckered her lips and shook her head back and forth.

"That's not nice, Charlie," Ramona replied becoming agitated as she tugged on her long hair pulling it up in its ponytail. "Jeffery is just different from everyone that's all, he's – so dreamy."

"Dreamy, oh please," Charlie chided with her voice rising. "You sound like my mom. She brought Jeffery up just a little while ago. You two are just plain crazy. Jeffery is an uppity dipshit."

"Charlie, watch your mouth. He's misunderstood that's all," Ramona added She leaned back on her elbows looking up through the trees. "Oh," she moaned, "he has those hazel eyes and such broad shoulders."

"Boy, you have it bad. Jeffery is a snobbish fool and the whole Montgomery family is like him, oh except Carol, now she's nice."

"Charlie," Ramona frowned swinging her head to look at Charlie.

"Sorry Ramona, enough talk, let's get wet," Charlie called out leaping up from the cool grass squealing with delight as she jumped into the chilly spring pool making a big splash.

"Charlie, wait!" Ramona yelled. She stood. Her shorts slipped off and she carefully laid them to the side so they didn't get torn or dirty, just as she did each time when the girls were alone.

Charlie's face tensed. How could life be so unfair? She knew Ramona was so poor and didn't have many pairs of shorts.

Ramona jumped in the cool water. "Oh, this feels good!" Ramona squealed.

The splash brought Charlie back from her thoughts.

Ramona turned to Charlie, her face crinkled and her head shook no. She didn't want pity for being poor.

"The water is getting low and we need to get that one rock in place. Do you think Jessie is still helping your father?" asked Charlie.

"No," came a familiar voice from behind her.

Startled, Charlie spun around and looked up.

"Jessie, I thought you were working out in the field with Poppa?" questioned Ramona. She leaned back her arms out wide floating, but her eyes stared up at her brother.

Jessie stood tall, very handsome with the same long blonde hair and blue eyes just as she had.

"I was, but Poppa wasn't feeling well. He got too hot out in the field, so we stopped. I thought I'd take a swim and cool off. I should've known you two would be here," he said chuckling. His eyes squinted at the two girls as he smoothed his long, wild blonde hair away from his face.

He gasped! "Ramona! You took your shorts off again. What if someone else came down here?" he snapped, as he pulled his shirt off laying it over by her shorts. "One of the workers from the back fields of Bella Oak might come down this way, even on a Sunday."

Jessie stopped moving. His mouth puckered, peering down at the two girls. "You know Hudson has been hanging around. He's just white trash. He's a sorry, low life piece of shit and could be dangerous. Even the people from the bottoms have chased him away. You need to be more careful when you come down here."

"Mom told me earlier he's hanging around and he'll be sorry if he comes near us," said Charlie in a sharp voice scrunching her face.

"I heard from Billy Mac," Jessie continued, "Hudson was stealing from the bottoms and he said the law is after him for raping one of the girls over in Jackson County."

"Well, one day last year I saw him up close and he was filthy and stunk," Charlie commented. "His dark eyes were staring at me giving me the creeps. Daddy told him to stay off Bella Oak property or he'd get shot," she added looking up at Jessie.

Jessie took a deep breath and looked down at Charlie's pistol sitting by the bank knowing Charlie was capable of using it. Ramona knew how to shoot the pistol, but she'd never hurt anyone. However, he knew Charlie wouldn't hesitate and the girls together would be fine.

"Well, girl, you keep that peashooter near you when you're down here and Ramona you wait near the house until Charlie gets here and stop coming down here on your own. She can yell up at you when she gets near the creek."

"Okay, I'll be more careful." Ramona ducked her head down shaking it to the side, "but Jessie. I can't swim in those shorts and mess up another pair. Your jean shorts are still too big…the ones mama gave me to wear," Ramona spoke softly her blue eyes looking up at her brother.

Jessie sighed. His hands clutch into fist tightening his fingers letting his nails bite into his hands, hating being poor. Ramona's face smiled back up at her brother wanting to take the pain from him. Being poor didn't bother her as it did Jessie. The old Jessie emerged, seeing Ramona so full of life not wasting her time worrying that she didn't have money or clothes.

"Geronimo!" yelled Jessie laughing making a huge splash in the cool water by the two girls. "Wow, you two did good damming up the creek, this is nice."

"Alright," Charlie announced her face beamed proud at the compliment. "Now that you're here you can help us move the last rock to finish damming up the spring, especially before tomorrow and everyone splashes out all the water."

"I'll help directly. This water is so cold," he said. Jessie took in a deep breath going under the water for a second and then he lay back floating arms out wide on the water. "Is everyone coming to the picnic this year?"

"Yes," Ramona admitted. "This picnic is going to be wonderful and you could also be nice to Jeffery. Oh," she teased laughing, "Sharon'll be here too."

"Sharon is too snooty. She's just like you Red," Jessie answered looking over at Charlie. Red was the nickname he gave

Charlie when they were little and it stuck since her hair had even became redder the older she became. He stealthy began swimming closer to the girls silently reaching out his arms to dunk them both.

"I'm not snooty," said Charlie, her red ponytail swished in the water. She grinned as she splashed Jessie back not letting him get near, always winning the sneak attack, calculating Jessie's move, just as she had done their entire lives.

"Yea, right. You living up there in that gigantic home, on the largest and wealthiest plantation in these parts," he added. He stopped talking, not pushing her too far, not wanting to rile her up. She did have a quick temper. He knew she was as tough as nails.

His blue eyes became intense watching her every move, even more than normal. It'd become harder for him to hide his inter thoughts of Charlie, thoughts that had grown over the years. Okay, is that the rock you two rolled down from the hill? You couldn't have found a smaller one?"

"That rock is just right. I picked it out," said Charlie briskly. She grabbed the limb hanging down on the side of the bank, the one that they used for years to climb out of the spring. Her other hand squeezed her red ponytail as she pulled herself out of the water.

"Red, does your Dad know what you are doing?" Jessie asked lying back floating with his eyes following her very closely.

Charlie stood on the bank. Water dripped off her body making her wet t-shirt fit tight around her breast, not making Jessie's hidden dreams any easier.

"Yes, I think so, I haven't talked to Daddy, but it's okay, Joshua has been down here shooting some moccasins. He says there've been a few more snakes than normal. So, he's seen the dam and hasn't said anything."

Charlie paused, taking a deep breath, studying the creek. "It'll work just fine," she added justifying her work. "If we could just get that last Gawd damn rock moved!" she squealed wiggling her hands on her hips impatiently waiting for Jessie to climb out of the water. Her green eyes narrowed staring down into Jessie's blue eyes.

"Charlie," Ramona called out, "stop cussing."

"Alright, don't get your feathers in a ruffle. I'm fixing to help as long as I don't get in trouble," Jessie assured. He understood how hardheaded Charlie was. Always given in, he grabbed a hold of the limb carefully climbing out of the creek.

Jessie stared down at the young girl he'd loved his entire life. He'd been able to hide his feeling for all these years, but it was getting harder each day. He stood not moving. Thoughts were swirling in his mind as he looked into her green eyes. He knew he wasn't right for her, a poor boy from a small farm. He also knew she had her own dreams for her future and he wasn't a part of them and he'd never be.

Charlie stood proud as she watched Jessie understanding she was getting her way.

"Ramona, you stay in the water," Jessie called back. "I don't want to see you in your panties. Mom'd have a fit if she knew you were swimming like that. Red and I can get this." He shook his head making his blonde hair fly back and forth.

"You ain't going to tell on me," Ramona begged, "are you? I don't want to hurt Momma's feelings."

"No, just calm down, come on Red push. You had to find the largest rock around here."

"It's gonna fit perfect," Charlie declared, leaning over by the rock, "I measured."

"If you say so." He shrugged his shoulders, scooting in next to her.

They gave a good push and the rock rolled down the hill landing in between the two rocks splashing in the clear water fitting just right.

"See," squealed Charlie. She looked up at Jessie standing close who was a year and a half older than she was. She became quiet.

He took in a deep breath bringing his composure back. "You two need to be careful if old Joshua has been killing snakes down here. They're coming to the water since it's been so hot and dry. Now, you both keep a watch out for Hudson. I'll be up on the hill drawing, if you need me," Jessie added, picking up his shirt and turning to leave.

"Thanks Jessie," Charlie called back.

"No problem, Red," Jessie yelled back, waving his shirt in the air disappearing over the hill.

Charlie sat down on the cool ground pulling her knees up to her chest. She reached around them with her arms rocking back and forth.

"Have you seen any of his drawings?" she asked.

Jessie had drawn in tablets her entire life, but she hadn't thought about what he could be drawing, until now. Her inquisitiveness of Jessie seemed to be growing for some odd reason.

"Nope."

"He sure does sit and draw a lot; I wonder what his drawings look like and I would love to see some."

"I've seen a few pictures that he's drawn of Momma and Poppa, but I haven't seen any others. He has tablet after tablet hidden in his room."

"He sure has been secretive about them," Charlie's voice drifted off with thoughts of Jessie and his tablets. She wiggled her head, and then turned and looked back up the hill.

"Now, back to tomorrow." Ramona interrupted. "Alright, I wish I had something new to wear this fourth." She moaned pointing her head to the side. "Those are my best shorts."

"How about wearing my dark blue shorts with that bluish tie die shirt you made at church last month, my mom won't care if you borrow my shorts."

Ramona sighed, taking in a deep breath. She sat there for a second letting her long hair dripped with water. "But, you know my momma won't like me borrowing your clothes and Poppa'd be mad."

"Ramona, stop puckering you face, it's gonna stay that way. You'd be fine wearing my shorts. No one's gonna care."

"I don't know, if I should," Ramona moaned in a soft voice.

"Now I think," Charlie interjected before Ramona could say anything else. "My blue, two piece swim suit will be perfect for you." She chuckled. "It'll fit you better than me with your curves…." She moaned. "If you want to get Jeffery's attention."

"Charlie, stop teasing. I'm not that curvy. You ain't going to embarrass me tomorrow, are you?" Ramona asked timidly.

"No, I swear I won't embarrass you." Charlie chuckled stretching her legs out straight. Her head tilted to the side. "But, you do have a better shape than me. Stop giving me that look, I said I promise and I'll be good."

"I've gotta help Momma with some canning in the morning, but I'll be over as soon as I'm done," said Ramona jumping up from the grassy bank. "I better get home, it's getting late, and I promised Momma to help with supper." She stopped and heaved a sigh. "Oh, I can't wait until tomorrow, I'm so nervous."

"Ramona, you're just a worry wart. This is going to be the best picnic, just you wait and see," Charlie reassured. She leaned back on the cool grass staring up into the trees watching a squirrel leaping from limb to limb. He stopped, wiggled, and barked at her.

Ramona squeezed her long blond hair and then she shook her shorts and slipped them on. "Bye, Charlie, you be careful staying here by yourself and watch for snakes."

"I'll be okay. See you tomorrow," Charlie called out. She didn't move taking in a deep breath of the clean summer air. Her hand reached over feeling her peashooter lying by her side. "Anyway, Jessie ain't far up on his hill, drawing his pictures," she yelled.

CHAPTER 3

July 4th

Early the next morning, the light from the morning sun flickered from the twisted oak's limbs that were outside her bedroom window giving off shadows across her room. The small, warm breeze from the open window gently blew the pink ruffled curtains framing the window showing that this Fourth of July was going to be another hot, dry day.

Charlie picked up her new two-piece red polka dot bathing suit, the one her mom had bought on her last shopping trip in Charleston. She slipped her gown and panties off. She quickly tied the bathing suit's string around her neck, fastened the top and pulled the bottom of the bathing suit up.

She shook her head as she stared at the reflection in the mirror over her dresser seeing her long body with small breast and straight figure. She laughed looking at her wild, curly red hair that she'd inherited from her grandmother Charlene, her daddy's momma, who she was named after. She'd been told she had the same temper and spirit of her grandmother Charlene, along with the hardheadedness, a very shrewd woman. Charlie was also was named after Olivia Bellamead, who'd saved Bella Oak from the Yankees when they tried to burn her during the civil war. Two strong women and Charlie got the best of both. Her freckles, that ran across her nose, were all her own and she couldn't blame anyone for them. Her face was long and pointed, knowing she looked like her father green eyes and all, a true Bellamead. But, she was more of her mother's size, not very big with long skinny legs.

She slipped her white shorts and wild flowered top over her bathing suit. Okay, she stared in the mirror; she was ready for the Fourth of July party that would be starting in a few hours. She raced down the long staircase.

"Good morning, Charlene," excitedly said Martha turning around from the kitchen sink waving her dripping hands in the air. "I'm glad you're up early. You can empty the ice trays into the container in the freezer and refill them. It's already hotter than a firecracker this morning, so we'll use a lot of ice today."

Pearl, a large black woman, stood over the hot gas stove baking her fried apple pies making the kitchen smothering hot. The lone, black oscillating fan in the corner of the kitchen slowly swished back and forth sending the smell of fresh baked pies floating throughout the home.

Charlie opened the refrigerator. She didn't move for a few seconds feeling the cool air on her face, finally she gave in pulling the trays of ice from the freezer.

"Pearl, the pies smell great," she said leaving the door of the freezer slightly open as she squeezed the plastic trays with the ice falling into the large container.

"Thanks sweetie, but you never know," answered Pearl. The same answer she always used each year for Charlie's life, knowing the pies were the best in the county.

"Can I have one for breakfast? I love 'em when they're fresh and hot," asked Charlie putting the filled water trays back into the freezer. She reluctantly closed the freezer's door.

"Shor', come on over. I need someone to sample one, since Joshua isn't here to taste them," proclaimed Pearl proudly. "Here's ya a glass of cold milk."

Joshua and his wife Pearl had been married thirty-five years and lived in the small farmhouse out back of the huge plantation home all of Charlie's life. Joshua, who was a few years older than her father, was born in that same old farmhouse outback and he'd grown up there, never leaving, just as his father before him. He was now the Foreman for the plantation, but to Charlie and her parents he was family.

Pearl stood anxiously with her arms crossed like a nervous contestant looking at a judge while Charlie took the first bite of the fresh fried pie. When Charlie moaned scrunching up her mouth a big smile came on Pearl's face.

"As good as ever, maybe better this year, the dried apples have a little more flavor," answered Charlie giving her critique.

"Mom, what else do you need me to do?" she asked, as she finished up the last sip of milk and bite of fried pie.

"When Ramona gets here, see if she can get Jessie to come over and help set up the tables under the old oak for me," announce Martha turning around pulling out the freshly ironed tablecloths from the large pantry. "Your daddy and Joshua are going to be too hot and tired when they finish plowing the field and we've got a heap of work to do."

"They shor' are and I hope the heat doesn't make 'em sick. It was hard on 'em yesterday, they were plum tuckered out," Pearl offered worriedly. Her eyes peered down at her fried pies as she wiped her hands on her apron. "I reckon this heat is staying for a while."

The old woman shook her head and turned to the hot stove slowly dropping more pies into the boiling black pot sending hot steam into the room.

Charlie put her empty plate and glass in the sink full of sudsy water washing them and setting them in the drain board to dry. "Ramona has to help her mom this morning, so I'll go and get Jessie."

"That'd be great," her mom added, busily stacking all of the dishes on the kitchen table from the cabinets.

"I'll be back in a little while."

Charlie stopped before she went out the door and reached over with a paper napkin grabbing a fried pie. "A bribe always works on Jessie," she said grinning.

Pearl chuckled. "Yes r re that boy will do anything for a fried pie."

The old kitchen screen door squeaked, slamming shut. "Sorry," Charlie called back before Pearl could get onto her. She carefully stepped over ole Betsy; the dog looked up sleepily and yawned at her. Ole Betsy, her daddy's ole hound dog, always lay by the back steps in a hole she'd dug out years ago, and Joshua and her daddy had let it go.

The morning was quiet. Charlie stepped into her and Ramona's remarkable world of the spring creek. She didn't budge hearing a crunching sound of dried leaves a few feet behind her. Her heart hammered in her chest. Her defenses took over. She spun around catching a glimpse of someone hiding behind a tree. She knew it was that yellow belly scalawag, Hudson. She reached down grabbing her pistol. She carefully slipped the fried pie down into her holster. Most girls would have screamed, but not her, she'd take care of that low life.

"Alright you bastard, you better get the hell off of Bella Oak!" Charlie yelled.

She waved with her hand trembling her pistol in the air. Not backing down, she listened to what was around her as she gripped tight her pistol. She felt the stare of his eyes, and heard the crunch on the leaves getting closer. She couldn't see him, but she could smell a disgusting order and knew he was getting near. Her fingers tightened their grip on the pistol. Her body tensed. She pondered the stories about Hudson and the young girls, and knew that she wasn't going to be one. Her body stiffened. Her eyes scanned the woods for any sign. The pistol cocked, but…

Hudson grabbed her from behind and with his right hand he wrapped tight his fingers over her mouth. She spun around and was face to face with the horrible man. His eyes narrowed and a smile emerged on his filthy face showing missing front teeth. He pulled her close. She gagged. His body reeked of sweat, and ale.

Her gun slammed into his chest. He froze. Her finger twitched on the trigger, but not fast enough. His left hand flew in the air and the gun sailed out of her hand to the ground landing in a pile of leaves a few feet away. Her screams were muffled resonating through his hand that was tightly clasped over her mouth. He held her securely bringing her body next to his.

Hudson's eyes moved along her body, ready for his hands to take over. "Frisky, I like feisty girls. You're different from most of the girls around here and I like a challenge. I'm fixing to have me a rich girl," he grunted, "a southern belle," he said pompously letting out an eerie laugh. "I ain't ever had one like you, before."

Charlie fought without success. However, her knee slammed him with a direct hit between his legs right in the balls. His body bowed over in excruciating pain.

"You high-falutin bitch," he mumbled. His cold glazed-over eyes stared down at her. His hands continued to grip her arms and mouth even tighter.

She prepared for another good hit. He couldn't stop her legs from kicking, however...

His face paled. His eyes stared behind her with a terrified gaze. His hand fell from her mouth, he let go of his grip around her waist, and then he knocked her to the ground.

He shouted, "Who are you? Get the hell away from me, you can have the bitch!"

Charlie lay on the ground staring up at the wild man. See looked over seeing her gun lay a few feet from her. She scooted on the ground and her hand reached to retrieve her pistol. She gripped the peashooter in her hand, and pulled herself up on her knees. She twirled around in a half circle with the pistol cocked in her hand ready to fire. But, Hudson was already weaving through the trees not leaving her a clear shot. She shook her head. She could see a shadow or silhouette of another person chasing after Hudson. She stared through the trees wondering if it her daddy or Joshua had heard the ruckus. However, that couldn't be. She could hear the tractor's motors in the field. Alright, who could have frightened a man like Hudson enough to run away like a little girl who had just saw a ghost?

She didn't move. Her eyes watched for any sign of Hudson.

"Dagnabbit," she yelled, swinging her pistol in the air. "Next time you son of a bitch, ya ain't getting away." She pulled the wrapped fried pie out and replaced her pistol in its holster. She knew that man wouldn't be back for a while. He was petrified of whoever was there. Nonetheless, she'd have her day meeting that man again. Her hand felt her pistol against her leg as she walked up the hill. She stopped. She raised her other hand in the air. *"That man will never touch me again and I won't hesitate next time pulling the trigger."*

Charlie wasn't given up. Her anger was growing. She ran along the path to the spring carefully stepping from rock to rock on the homemade dam. Her eyes were still on fire from the anger she'd felt. She stopped at the top of the hill, remembering how it felt having that repulsive man holding onto her making her body shiver.

She took in a deep breath and stared up to the top of the hill. Ramona and Jessie lived on twenty acres across Rock Creek from

Bella Oak. She knew Ramona and Jessie didn't like her to visit their home. They lived in a tiny planked home that was overflowing with kids. She sighed with relief when she saw Jessie sitting outside of the house in an old chair leaned against a tree holding his drawing tablet in his lap.

He looked up. His eyes became huge. The chair fell forward. A pencil swung in his hand. "Red, Ramona is in the house with Momma canning and she can't come out yet."

"I know, she told me she'd be over later, but Momma wanted me to come and see if you'd help set up the tables for the picnic. Daddy and Joshua are busy working in the field."

She carefully handed him the warm, freshly fried pie wrapped in the napkin. "Oh, here, this is from Pearl."

A big smile crossed his face. His tablet of drawings closed not giving her a chance to look at them. He took a jumbo bite of the warm pie and moaned with pleasure. He held his hand in the air trying to talk as he chewed the pie. "I'll be right back, gotta put my tablet away," he mumbled with his mouth full as he dashed across the yard to the house.

He came out the front door and took the last bite of pie. "Let's go," he yelled. "Pearl does know how to bake and I hope she has enough pies for everyone today," he said making his way to the creek bed.

"You don't have to worry about that. Pearl has been baking for hours and she always has plenty and she'll be happy for you to eat all you want," hollered Charlie, running behind him. "Slow down."

"Sorry Red, I forgot you have short legs," said Jessie as he slowed his pace on the slope of the hill. He stopped and watched her red hair flying in the air as she came near him.

"I don't have short legs, you just have very long legs," she yelled back. It was as if all of a sudden the past year, Jessie had grown so much taller than she had.

"Jessie, you didn't happen to chase down that ole Hudson a little while ago, did you?"

He spun around facing her.

"No, I ain't seen him or I wouldn't have just chased him I'd have caught him. Why!"

"That scalawag snuck up on me down by the spring and grabbed me, knocking my pistol out of my hand." She shivered. "It was so disgusting when he put his hands on me."

"What!" he shouted, "Why didn't you yell? Are you are right?" He grabbed her shoulders spinning her around to face him bringing her close. His face grimaced.

"Yes, I'm okay, stop worrying."

"Dammit Red you take to many chances. Where is he? How did you get away?"

"I'm shor' he is way gone by now. I kicked him in the balls with my knee and he bent over, but that didn't scare him away. It was strange he yelled at someone standing behind me. It was someone that terrified him. It was as if he saw a ghost or something and then he let me go. Whoever it was didn't say anything, but scared the fire out of that man. Hudson ran before I could get my pistol off the ground, so I didn't get a clear shot to shoot him or see who was chasing him. If it wasn't you that scared him away, then who chased him and who saved me?"

"I don't know who chased him away, but I'm sure glad they did. You keep that peashooter ready, if you hear anything give it to me. I'll be glad to put that sorry ass out of his misery," Jessie demanded making tight fists with his hands.

"I'll take care of that son of a bitch! I just wanted to let you know he was around this morning," she said laying her hand on her pistol that was hanging on her side. "You don't have to worry about me." She yelled as she darted down the hill to the creek's water. "I won't have him following me around and he'll never touch me again, next time he'll be sorry."

"You jus' be careful Red that was to close. You and Ramona don't need to be walking around down here alone. But, you don't have to worry about getting him. I'm going to take care of that white trash. I swear he'll never put his filthy hands on you again!"

"We'll get him Jessie, stop fretting, I'm fine. Now, we need to get Bella Oak ready for the picnic."

He nodded his head agreeing, but his eyes were telling a different answer. That despicable low life would never get near her again. He'd kill him first.

"I guess there haven't been any cancellations for the picnic and everyone'll be here today?" he questioned. He stepped on the rocks of the new dam, making his way across the creek.

"No cancellations, unfortunately Jeffery will be here and so will Vanessa, who you like." She stopped walking and turned toward him with her face scrunched into a frown. "Remember, she's a real girl, not a tomboy like me."

"You don't forget anything do you Red. I was teasing you about Vanessa. I jus' wanted to rile you up that was all. I don't like her, she's too prissy and she can't get dirty or mess up that hair. Maybe we can dunk her underwater when we go swimming and ruin that bouffant hairdo that she wears on top of her head. I wonder if it'd deflate like a balloon," he said laughing.

"Jessie Lee Ledford you're going to get us in trouble, but it sounds fun to me."

"Well," Jessie said becoming solemn. His eyes peered down at her. "You know Jeffery will be after you. He's like white on rice around you and ain't giving up on getting married as soon as you graduate. You're all he talks about at school. He thinks it's all set in stone and he's won. He's got his own dream of moving into Bella Oak." Jessie watched her reaction. His face quickly turned to the side, trying to hide his feelings. It'd become difficult for him not to show his envy of Jeffery, a wealthy plantation owner's son.

"Oh, I can deal with Jeffery and he can have all the plans he wants, but I have my own dreams," she answered. She looked up at Jessie, wondering why he was bringing up Jeffery. She smiled hearing a hint of jealousy in his voice. "But I'm more worried about Jeffery hurting Ramona."

Jessie didn't answer he just took long strides up the hill to the large house. He slowed his pace looking over at Charlie a few feet behind him.

Before they made it to the back of the plantation home, Charlie ran.

"Jessie," Charlie whispered turning her head back at him as she dashed to the smokehouse. "I think I saw Hudson."

"Red," Jessie called back, "wait!" He raced after her, but she vanished behind the smokehouse. Before he made it to the smokehouse, a shot rang out. He gasped and his heartbeat wildly in his chest as his breath was taken from his lungs.

Finally, Charlie walked out from behind the smokehouse. He sighed relieved as he breathed in a deep breath.

Alright!" Charlie yelled, waving her pistol in the air, "I think I got him."

Jessie grabbed the pistol from her hand. "Dang it Red, slow down and wait for me next time," he yelled giving her a chastising look.

"Charlie," yelled Everett running from the backfield sweat dripping down his tired and dirty face. "What in the Sam hill is going   on?"

"Daddy," Charlie yelled back, "it was Hudson. I saw him stealing some meat from the shed. I think I got him. Dagnabbit." She looked back at the shed, shaking her head with her ponytail flying. "But, not good enough though, he got away."

"Yep, she must of hit him Mr. Bellamead, he's bleeding," Jessie called out, "Red, you need to tell your daddy about Hudson this morning."

"Next time girl you call me or Joshua and don't go chasing that man without us. Now what is Jessie talking about?" her daddy question wiping his brow with his handkerchief.

"Oh," she began, "I'm fine Daddy. It's just Hudson grabbed me this morning down by the creek. He's the vilest person and stunk making me nauseated."

"What! Young lady!" Everett yelled.

"He knocked my pistol out of my hand and I didn't get a chance to shoot him. Someone scared him off and he let me go. I don't know who it was. I didn't see anyone. Maybe it was one of the workers from the back field."

"Gawd dammit!" Everett yelled, "I knew I should've killed him last year when I had the chance. You be more careful and stop running around everywhere by yourself," he blurted out with his hand rubbing his gun on his side. "You don't go after him, again."

" Daddy, Jessie was with me this time. I was fine, but next time I won't miss," she confessed confidently.

"Red, we better go see your mom and Pearl, we need to get to work," Jessie said grabbing a hold of her hand. "Mr. Bellamead that bastard won't come near her as long as I'm around."

"You keep an eye on her Jessie and Charlie, you try and stay out of trouble," Everett insisted, grinning back at his daughter, a true spitfire.

Jessie smiled back at Everett nodding his head, knowing he couldn't keep Charlie out of trouble. Joshua and her daddy always said it must be that red hair, understanding she wasn't afraid of the devil.

"Good," Pearl called out from the kitchen window, "Jessie's here. What in heaven's name was going on out there?"

"Oh, Charlie shot Hudson, but it looked like she only nicked him and he was able to get away," Jessie replied.

"What!" Martha screamed in a high voice in the kitchen, "Charlene Olivia Bellamead, you let your daddy see to that man!"

"Yes, Ma'am," Charlie answered knowing she'd shoot that man again if she got the opportunity and next time she wouldn't miss.

"Jessie, the tables are outback. Joshua got them out of the barn, but didn't have time to set them up," said Pearl letting the screen door close behind her stepping out onto the back steps. She stopped wiped her hands on her apron and looked back as she grinned at Charlie

"We'll get everything done and thanks Pearl for the pie, their delicious as always," Jessie called back.

Pearl didn't move. She just stood by the kitchen door with her arms crossed and a big smile on her face.

The side yard began to look just as it did each year with lines of tables covered in long flowery tablecloths and stacks of plates sitting under the one large old, moss draped oak.

"That is perfect," Martha added walking around the yard nervously squeezing her hands together. "Now, the verandah needs to be done," she announced looking over at the two young people.

"Okay, come on Jessie you can help since Ramona isn't here yet. I'll sweep and you can blow up the balloons since you're so full of hot air," shouted Charlie running ahead of him.

"You're trying to kill me with all of the dust?" hollered Jessie coughing, swishing his arms in the air.

"Sorry, but it's so dry. It ain't working is it?" Charlie asked leaning on the broom, looking at the dust fly across the verandah.

"No," he said laughing letting one of the balloons soar into the air at her.

Jessie finished blowing up the last balloon and tied all the banners to the wooden white rail around the verandah, red, white, and blue beginning to be the theme. He then placed the American flag in its special spot by the front steps.

"Boy, this is a large verandah and a huge house," he said looking down at the other end of the long porch. "I forget how big this place is until each time I'm here," he added shaking his head, peering up at the tall ceiling watching the ceiling fans twirl in a circle.

"Don't say it," Charlie interrupted him, "that I'm a spoiled rich girl."

"I wasn't," he answered smiling down on her with his blue eyes.

"Hey, things look good, you two did a good job," came a voice from the side of the house. Ramona leaped up the steps. "Now," Ramona beamed, "it's really the fourth. Bella Oak is dressed like a true southern belle."

"Okay Ramona, let's get you changed into your shorts and swim suit, it's getting late," Charlie insisted grabbing the handle of the screen door.

Ramona puckered her mouth. She didn't move and her sad blue eyes looked up at her brother.

"Get dressed and I'm going to the kitchen to see if Red's mom or Pearl needs my help." Jessie grinned and gave Ramona a wink, a sign they'd used their entire lives that things would be okay.

CHAPTER 4

Friends

Charlie finished braiding Ramona's long blonde hair and laid the herringbone handle hairbrush on the dresser.

"You look great," Charlie assured. "I knew that bathing suit would fit you better than me," she chucked, "since you fill it out."

"Now – Charlie, you're not going to embarrass me – you promised," Ramona, begged, wiggling getting use to the bathing suit as she slipped the blue shorts over the swimsuit.

"I promise I'll be good."

Ramona peered out the window. "C'mon, the Montgomery's dark green Cadillac is pulling up behind Mr. Baxter's black Chevy Impala. We need to hurry downstairs."

The girls slid to a stop on the verandah.

Twins Sharon and Leann Baxter stepped out of Mr. Baxter's car and looked around.

Jeffery Montgomery opened the door to the Cadillac. He stood full of self-confidence helping his younger sister Carol out of the car. Jeffery smiled. His eyes stared up at the old plantation home seeing his dream in front of him of becoming the new owner of the plantation, believing he'd won Charlie.

The Dawson's red Lincoln Continental parked behind Mr.

Montgomery's Cadillac. Vanessa Dawson slid out of the back seat, her shining pink manicured nails reached up touching her light brown, beehive hair.

Chandler Dawson, a huge football player, followed Vanessa across the yard tucking his nervous hands in his pockets of his cutoff jeans, a true opposite of his sister. He stepped up on the verandah with his eyes fixed on Ramona. He blushed. His chubby cheeks turned a crimson red and his head ducked showing his hidden dreams.

The three Tolleson boys that Everett had hired were busy lining all the cars and trucks in the grassy area near the long tree lined drive leading to the house. Couples carrying blankets and folding chairs were getting situated all around the vast yard along with little ones running squealing with delight making the old plantation come alive.

The governor's car drove up the drive with its American flags flapping in the breeze stuck on the front of the car. The fat baldheaded man smiled and his arm waved out of the car window, always a politician. The long black car parked in front of the verandah.

The small band that was dressed in red, white, and blue stripped shirts and white pants was setting up their instruments on the small stage sitting in the middle of the circular drive by the huge magnolia tree.

The governor stepped from his car, waved to the people that were gathered in the front yard. He reached out his hand and greeted everyone as he made his way up to the verandah. Everett stood proud on the top step of the verandah. His hand shook the governor's hand and the band began to play *Dixie,* not wasting any time to get this picnic underway.

Everyone sang. *I wish I was in the land of cotton, old times there are not forgotten; Look away! Look away! Look away! Dixie's Land!*

The music flowed loudly echoing over the rolling hills full of tall South Carolina pines and old live oaks. The plantation was coming to life. This wasn't only a celebration for the United States but for the old south. Charlie stood staring at all of the people standing in the yard under the old moss draped oaks. The older people were gazing up at the aged home showing pride growing on their faces. Most of them had been here each Fourth of July picnic since they were babies. This was a tradition for the county, the state.

Charlie, a true southern girl, finished singing Dixie. She puffed up just as her father; this antebellum home was her pride and joy, a twinge of remorse hit her not wanting to leave Bella Oak.

Jessie stood by the veranda. His body tightened, eyes pierced as he watched the wealthy kids from the largest plantations in the county sitting on one end of the verandah. This maybe the 1960's, but life hadn't changed around these parts. The wealthy families of the south wanted to keep the bloodlines intact. They bred their children just as they did their horses.

Jeffery sat in the swing. His eyes on Charlie who was sitting on the porch floor by Ramona believing he'd won her and this plantation, the perfect social marriage for both families. Jeffery smirked. His eyes turned to Jessie telling Jessie he didn't have a chance with Charlie. It'd become hard the last year for Jessie to hide his feelings for Charlie since Jeffery had found out his hidden secret, taunting him, every chance he could about Charlie. Letting Jessie know that he'd won and Jessie didn't have a snowballs chance in hell with Charlie.

Jessie had to smile when he looked to the side of the verandah. There standing by the porch railing was Carol Montgomery trying not to let her brother Jeffery see who she was looking at. She cautiously watched Billy Mac Tolleson, a boy who lived on a small farm north of the Montgomery plantation. Carol's life was planned out for her like the rest of wealthy kids and she was supposed to marry a congressional representative's son from Colombia after she graduated high school.

Each one of the parents had planned their children's lives and Jessie knew he, Ramona and Billy Mac wasn't a part of the plan. They could be friends, but they wouldn't blend their genes with the wealthy.

He looked over at his sister Ramona. He sighed, knowing her dream of marrying and living on a plantation wouldn't come about, and his hidden dreams of Charlie, wouldn't become a reality either. All of their hidden dream would stay hidden.

He looked down at Charlie sitting on the old plank floor talking to everyone. Her red, bushy ponytail swung back and forth. Pain stabbed at his heart. His dream of a life with Charlie would never be.

Charlie felt the stare of Jessie's blue eyes. Her head swung upward and a smile emerged on her face.

The old iron bell that was used in the past to call the slaves in for lunch, began ringing telling everyone the barbecue was ready. The smell of the slow roasted meat filled the air. Everyone hurriedly found seats under the shade of the old twisted oak trees and out across the yard on multicolored quilts.

Miss Ethel and her group of blabbermouths gathered at one end of a table not missing a beat as they continued to gossip. Charlie smiled to herself; Myrtle Mae had been saved today by the story of Ed Hudson, now becoming the topic of gossip of all the women from the county.

As everyone finished eating the pork barbeque, coleslaw, baked beans, and southern potatoes, Jeffery quietly moved over and squatted down next to Charlie. He gently reached over taking her hand in the palm of his hand. "Let's go and see what you've done down at the creek. We need to hurry before the Governor decides to make his long winded speech – it has to be cooler down there."

Charlie stood from the table. Jeffery slipped his arm around her waist bringing her near. Close enough that she could feel his body breathing and smell his cologne. She turned around looking across the table at Jessie. His eyes squinted and the grin on his face disappeared as he ducked his head.

When they neared Rock Creek Charlie and the girls stopped walking. Jessie continued leading the boys, including the Tolleson boys, down the path through the thick woods to the spring.

The giggling girls followed Charlie to a special clump of old trees deeper in the forest. Each girl carefully slipped off their shorts and tops, laying them on an old stump, revealing their new bathing suits and hurried back down the path.

"I bet that water is cold," Chandler replied, taking his shirt off laying it to the side. He squatted down by the edge of the creek swishing his fingers around in the cool water.

Suddenly, Jeffery laughed and shoved Chandler into the swimming hole making a huge splash. Chandler popped up out of the water slinging his head back and forth with his eyes glaring at Jeffery.

Jeffery squatted down by the water still laughing at Chandler.

Ramona walked up next to Jessie and stared at Jeffery.

"Hey look, the white trash is wearing a bathing suit this year, not her old worn out shorts," Jeffery called out scowling at Ramona. "I wonder who she stole the suit from," he yelled, snickering with a spiteful look on his face.

Chandler's eyes glowed with fury. Mad as a hornet his large hands grabbed a limb on the side of the spring and he climbed out of the water. No one was going to hurt Ramona, not with him around. He didn't care how poor she was, money didn't matter to that boy, and no one was going to call her white trash.

Charlie's temper flared as if her red hair was on fire. She swung her arms in the air and ran up to Jeffery.

"You dumb ass snobbish fool!" she shouted, giving him a push in the back with all of her strength knocking Jeffery into the pool of water, expensive boots, shirt, jeans, and all.

Ramona's small body trembled standing by the stream and tears ran down her face. She turned to run, but Chandler reached down and his large fingers gently wiped her tears. "C'mon Ramona let's go for a swim and have fun."

Jeffery was fuming as he climbed out of the water, his eyes squinted and his hands clenched making fists as he opened and closed them. He walked toward Charlie on a mission. No girl was going to get the best of him.

Jessie stepped in front of Charlie blocking Jeffery's path. Jeffery's tight-fisted hand swung in the air, but Jessie quickly put his left arm up blocking Jeffery's punch and Jessie's right fist punched Jeffery in the nose.

"You, white trash bastard! I'm taking you down!" Jeffery shouted.

Chandler took one long stride standing in front of Jessie. Jeffrey knew he couldn't fight Chandler. Charlie put her hand up in the air stopping the big guy letting Jeffery run past them up the hill.

Charlie smiled at Chandler and winked at Jessie. "I can see to things from here," she called back to the two boys. She turned darting after Jeffery up the hill and through the thick trees. She zipped past Jeffery who was holding his shirt on his bloody nose as he walked with his expensive boots squishing with each step.

Charlie ran ahead of Jessie to the verandah. She pushed the gardenia bushes aside by her father who was sitting next to the railing in one of the worn white rockers talking to the governor and a group of men.

"What's wrong, Charlie?" her daddy asked, leaning over the railing by her. Joshua scooted his chair close to listen. She moved some of the balloons and began her story of what Jeffery said to

Ramona and Jessie. Her father stood from the rocker with a look on his face you didn't see often. He was a kind gentle man but Jeffery had pushed him too far. He didn't have the quick temper of Charlie, but you didn't want to make him angry. She knew Mr. Montgomery always got his way, but not this time.

"Honey, you go back to the creek and swim. You tell Jessie the whole mess will be all right. I'll handle everything," he whispered, walking over to Zach Montgomery and Jeffery.

Charlie squatted down on the bank of the spring. "Where's Jessie?" she quietly asked Ramona.

"He left… Ohhhhhhh, Charlie, is he in trouble?" asked Ramona anxiously standing in the water next to Chandler.

"No, he isn't in trouble and I'm going to go get him," Charlie assured. "I think I know where he is."

Charlie raced in the hot sun up the creek's bank to the top of the hill. There, standing tall in front of her was the old twisted, massive oak tree that had to be hundreds and hundreds years old with its huge limbs resting gently and peacefully on the ground.

Just as she thought, Jessie was sitting quietly absorbed in his drawings on one of the enormous moss covered limbs lying on the ground. He didn't see or hear her as she came up from behind him. Her body froze. She could see what he was drawing – a picture of her…. She quietly took the picture in. Her eyes didn't blink staring at the sketch. It was the most incredible image of her sitting on the bank of the creek staring at the water flowing across the rock dam she'd built. The portrait was realistic and there was something enchanting about the drawing.

"Wow, that is great," she offered ducking under one of the low limbs turning around facing him.

He quickly closed the tablet.

"Don't close it," she begged sitting down next to him.

"I don't show anyone my drawings – sorry," he said nervously ducking his head down hiding his eyes from her.

"Well, put the tablet away and come back to the spring, we're going to have fun and you can't miss seeing Ramona with Chandler, they're both having the time of their lives….."

"Charlie," he paused, "Mr. Montgomery can get me into a heap of trouble."

"You ain't in trouble. If I'd gotten a chance, I'd punched Jeffery too. Daddy's handling everything," she assured grabbing a hold of his arm

"You shor', he's not gonna do something?"

"Yes, I'm sure, you are fine."

"Give me a minute," he said throwing his hand in the air. "I'll be right back," he shouted running up the hill to his house.

Charlie wondered what else Jessie had drawn? Now, she was curious of him and that curiosity wasn't going away. She watched him disappear over the hill, but before she could think anymore, he came running down the hill to the old tree his blonde hair flying in the wind.

"Let's go!" he shouted waving his arm to her. He slowed down his pace while she ran to catch up. When they made it to the spring, he smiled at Charlie. He stopped moving, staring down in the water at his sister. Ramona's face was glowing her eyes only seeing Chandler standing close to her, she didn't even notice them walking up.

"C'mon," Jessie declared reaching his arm around Charlie. He brought her close, jumping into the cool water making a big splash as they both screamed with delight.

Charlie couldn't stop her mind thinking about that one drawing, especially since Jessie's blue eyes stayed fixed on her for the rest of the day.

As the day finally came to an end Charlie and Ramona sat back in the swing on the verandah.

"Wow," Charlie moaned, pushing her bare feet on the porch letting the swing slowly move. "I'm bushed; this has been a long day and a lot of work. Listen to the katydids serenading the night it's so calming."

"Ohhhhhhh – this was the best fourth of July ever," Ramona beamed, giving Charlie every detail about Chandler over and over. "Okay, I admit you were right, Jeffery is a snobbish fool, and Chandler is so kind, thoughtful, understanding, considerate." Ramona kept babbling on and on finally stopping …. "Thank you for standing up for me today."

"That's what friends are for, and it was a great day wasn't it," Charlie replied.

Both girls leaned back in the swing. Charlie's red hair and Ramona's long blonde hair flowed with the movement of the swing.

"Ramona," called out Jessie looking up at the two girls, "we need to get home."

Charlie stopped the swing and started laughing. "What have you got in your pockets?"

"Pearl gave me a stack of fried pies for helping; this is the best payment ever," he answered, grinning with his blue eyes shining.

Ramona leaped down the steps. "Bye, Charlie I'll see you tomorrow."

"Bye Red," Jessie yelled back. The two of them disappeared down the path to the spring.

Charlie's mind wouldn't stop thinking about the day. She lay in her soft bed with the warm breeze blowing in the windows from the attic fan, gently moving the curtains. Finally she drifted off to a peaceful sleep.

CHAPTER 5

Feelings

The next morning Charlie looked in the mirror trying to figure out why she was at ease and so ready for the new day. The picnic had somehow changed her. Maybe it was seeing Ramona excited, finding someone that cared for her and she cared about. That was Ramona's dream staying in the county and living right here on a huge plantation. Chandler wasn't like the rest of the wealthy families and he didn't worry about social graces. He had his eyes on Ramona and nothing; not even his parents, were going to stop him from being with Ramona.

Charlie and Ramona had sat down on the bank of the old spring creek their entire lives telling each other their deepest secrets and dreams. And at least one of their dreams might come true. That had to be her answer.

She slipped on her jean shorts and her tie-dye multicolored shirt that she had made at church.

The kitchen was sweltering once more. Pearl busily stood over the gas stove canning some of the early tomatoes. As the tomatoes simmered in their pot on top of the stove, the lone oscillating fan swung back and forth filling the air with the sweetness of summer.

Charlie smiled when she heard her mom singing in the back yard hanging clothes on the clothesline.

"Good morning, sweetie pie," said Pearl wiping her moist face with her apron. "I have a chore for you this morning. We had a lot barbeque left from the picnic. So, I've fixed this basket for you to take to the Ledford's. We just don't have room for the food and they can use it." She started laughing. "I know Jessie'll make the most of all the food. I shor' don't know how that boy can eat so much and stay so skinny."

"Sure Pearl, I'll take it over in a few minutes. Do ya have an extra pie for me this morning?"

"Always, sweetie, I've already warmed one and here's your nice cold glass of milk," said Pearl smiling with her cheeks puffing on her round face. "It shore was a nice picnic yesterday, even with the episode with Jeffery. Don't tell Jessie, but I'm glad he got that boy good." She grunted. "Your mom thinks that Jeffery's a nice young man." Pearl shook her head. "But, I know different. That Jeffery is what gives plantation owners a bad name and he thinks he's too big for his britches. Saying those mean words to sweet Ramona, he's just ornery," she said bitterly, her small brown eyes sequenced. Pearl became quiet and busily turned back to the stove. "Everett shor; took care of that boy. Joshua said he was fit to be tied and he hadn't seen him that mad since he caught the Johnson boys stealing from old widow Smithson."

Charlie took a bite of the fried pie shaking her head agreeing with Pearl. She always loved it when Pearl would become riled up. One more bite and the warm pie was gone. She scooted her chair back from the table and reached over lifting the basket. "Wow, this is full! This should last them for a while. Thanks Pearl for the pie," she said gratefully, going over to the old wooden screen door.

"Now, ya don't let Mr. Ledford see you giving them that food," Pearl added puckering her lips together. "Mrs. Ledford won't have any problems with taking the leftovers, but he'll think its charity. I swear that man has too much pride and don't know about being neighborly, now hurry on your way and don't diddle daddle."

"Okay, I'll be careful and hide from Mr. Ledford."

Charlie struggled with the heavy basket pushing the screen door open, softly closing it. She stopped and looked downward. "Good morning, Betsy," she said carefully stepping over the sleeping dog, who looked up at her and yawned.

Charlie placed her right foot on the rock dam and made her way up to the small farmhouse. She stopped at the top of the hill. *"Oh, now what?"* she thought. She'd never been inside the tiny home. Her hands gripped tightly to the basket's handle and she took in a deep breath. Her hand softly knocked on the wooden screen door.

Mrs. Ledford walked up to the door with a surprised look on her face. "Charlie," she paused pushing opening the tattered screen door. "Ramona is busy right now and can't leave."

"I know, Mrs. Ledford, but Pearl and my mom sent this basket of leftovers from the picnic over to you. They've run out of freezer and refrigerator space," she added showing Mrs. Ledford the basket.

Something caught Charlie's eye and she quickly looked into the house. There sitting in a makeshift room above the kitchen with an old rickety ladder leaning by the wall. Jessie's blue eyes stared down on her. He quickly leaped to the floor from his room in the attic. The make shift loft was only about 4 foot tall. His head ducked and his face turned red. She understood why he called her a spoiled rich girl living in the large plantation home.

"Come in child, it's too hot out there in the sun," said Mrs. Ledford stepping back as she took the basket. "Here, let me empty the basket so you can take it home with you." The woman moved over to the tiny kitchen and sat the basket on the small kitchen table.

The blue-eyed baby girl Debbie sat on the floor next to the other two blonde haired boys, Billy and Bobby that were about six years old. One lone fan sat blowing hot air in the small house. The living room and kitchen together wasn't much bigger than her bedroom. She looked over and Jessie saw her looking around. His face bowed with shame as he ran out the back door. Ramona hurried, carrying an empty laundry basket in tow, past Jessie into the kitchen.

"Charlie, oh…wow that's a lot of food. It was good yesterday. Poppa will like that barbeque," she said helping her mom put the food away. "This is nice of Pearl and your mom."

"Well, you know Pearl always cooks way too much and we can't eat all of it and I know Jessie loves the barbeque and pies," Charlie added chattering too much.

Mrs. Ledford was thin, a very pretty woman with light brown hair full of blonde streaks. The real blonde hair of the children came from Mr. Ledford along with the blue eyes. Ramona and Jessie did have their mother's nose and shape of her face, a beautiful woman.

"There, that's it. You tell your mom and Pearl thank you, and we'll surely enjoy it, especially in this heat. Trying to cook makes the house so hot," Mrs. Ledford added kindly fanning her apron.

"I hope it rains soon and cools things off," said Charlie caringly, staring at Mrs. Ledford seeing how troubled she was.

"Well, honey this helps a heaping – having meat to go along with what vegetables we're getting from the garden, but our garden shor' is drying up." Nervously, Mrs. Ledford began to straighten up the kitchen.

"I'd better get back home and get my chores done. I'll see you later, Ramona," Charlie assured lifting the empty basket from the kitchen table.

"Thank you Charlie for bringing all of this food over," Mrs. Ledford called out, as Charlie opened the screen door stepping out into the hot sun.

She turned to go down to the Rock Creek swimming hole, but something was pulling her. She spun around and headed up stream to the huge old twisted live oak on the hill overlooking the creek and countryside. There, as she thought, sitting up high in the old gnarled tree was Jessie looking far off, absorbed in his drawing not hearing her come up.

"Jessie," she called out not wanting to surprise him. "Pearl sent you some more pies in the basket. You're her biggest fan you know."

She sat the empty wicker basket down by the trunk of the huge tree. She pulled herself up onto a large limb of the tree beneath Jessie. She pushed the hanging, brownish grey Spanish moss to the side.

"You tell her thank you for me," he answered looking down at the ground. He knew, the realization he wasn't good enough for her. The truth, his hidden dream would never become a reality. His head stayed turned from her trying to hide his feelings.

"You know I'm not going to live like this my whole life. I maybe country poor, but I'm sure not white trash like Jeffery said," He began apprehensively, picking at the small twigs on the tree. "I'm going to school and become an architect and move away from here and make a lot of money, and not live like my parents."

"I know you're not white trash!" Charlie shouted, grabbing a hold of a limb gripping it tightly. "And don't let Jeffery get to you! He is a dimwitted idiot – that doesn't know his ass from a hole in the ground!"

Jessie shook his head back and forth. He couldn't stay upset long around her. His head ducked and his eyes still looked at the ground, but a slight grin emerged on his face,

Charlie relaxed her grip on the limb. "You know Jessie? I'm not staying here either. I'm moving to Atlanta where the homes have air conditioning and real pools in their back yards – not creeks to swim in." She leaned back against the tree. "I'm going to travel, and I'm going to see New York and go as far as California.... I might even travel to Italy and France and not sit here like all of these people never venturing out of the county." Her voice trailed off, as she dreamed of faraway places.

Jessie finally laughed. "I guess you and I are a lot of alike, Red. Maybe, I'll see you in Atlanta sometime – maybe we can find a place to eat that makes good fried pies," he declared. His fingers smoothed back his long blonde hair from his face showing his blue eyes.

She smiled up at him.

"You know if you climb to the top of this tree," he softly began. He leaned back against the trunk of the tree peering up through the large crooked limbs seeing beams of light filtering through the limbs giving off shadows dancing around them. "You can see the next county all the way to the river, not far from the great Atlantic Ocean. It's amazing up there and a whole new world out there waiting for me to discover it. I'm going to travel too. One of these days – yep one of these days," he said with his voice getting quiet.

"It's nice sitting here in this old tree. It's amazing how huge its limbs are twisting and sticking out like arms pointing to world unknown. I wonder how old it is," she asked. Her eyes looked up at him watching the breeze blowing his untamed blonde hair.

"My Poppa said this tree could be close to at least seven hundred years old. It has set here near the creek protected by the woods to the southeast where most storms come in. It could tell us a lot of stories from the past. I betcha there've been a lot of others, probably some of you kin folks that've climbed up into the tree looking so far out to new worlds."

"I can't believe it could be that old, but it'd be neat to have it talk to us and tell us its stories," she said. "I hope you don't mind? I'd like to stay for a while."

"Sure, if you want," he said in a soft voice, leaning down to her. "Here," his hand reached down and she put her hand into his soft hand making her body tingled with an unfamiliar feeling. Her insides warmed as he tenderly squeezed her hand. "You need to move up to this limb," he said gently pulling her up next to him, bringing her very close.

"Jus' look over yonder, you can see down to the creek where it flows over the rocks making a small waterfall. There has been more animals coming since it's so dry, some raccoons, deer and I saw a red fox the other evening." He laughed. "It had a tail that looked like your hair especially when you pull your hair up in a ponytail and it dries after you've been swimming."

She was relieved that he had calmed down about his home and was teasing her again. Jessie and her daddy were the only two people that she let tease her and Jessie seemed to know how far he could push her. She settled onto the limb getting way to relaxed, emotions stirred inside of her feeling him quietly breathing next to her.

She gasped. "Oh, you're right; this is great. Now, I know why you come here all of the time. No wonder you draw so much," she added. She stared downhill watching water flow over a small waterfall in the creek, so quietly hearing only the whisper of noise from the water trickling along the rocks.

"Mr. Kent says you draw better than anyone he's ever seen.... Why don't you show anyone your work?" she inquired leaning back against the limb.

"I draw just for me and I know everyone would make fun of my drawings. I just can't show them – not yet"

"I'd love to see some of your drawings and I promise I won't make fun of them," she compassionately said getting way to comfortable looking into his caring eyes.

He tenderly leaned down by her his face only a few inches from hers with their eyes meeting. She couldn't move or didn't want to move. She stared into his blue eyes that'd been haunting her more and more. Jessie's hand tenderly touched her face as he pulled her close with their lips meeting. Her emotions were taking over and she'd never felt like this before. She closed her eyes listening to the wind rustle the leaves on the big tree. She felt Jessie's hand softly caress her neck. She wrapped her hands around his head, tenderly playing with his wild hair. She could feel the passion he had, not holding back his feeling.

Her body jolted. Now, she knew why she was so happy yesterday. It wasn't just Ramona finding someone, but her. She flinched, knowing she couldn't let herself fall in love with Jessie. She had to leave this small town and nothing was going to change her mind, and she wasn't for sure going to become a Myrtle Mae.

She pulled herself from Jessie. "I better get back home. I have my chores to do," she whispered her voice trailing off.

Charlie could handle anything or anyone, but this was something she didn't understand. She knew she had to get away from Jessie and not let her feelings take over. She grabbed the basket sitting on the bottom branch, but she stopped before she walked away. She turned back and peered up into the tree.

Jessie grinned.

She hurriedly crossed the dam on the old spring creek. She stopped next to the water and stared down at her reflection. "Oh, what's happening to me? I wish you could tell me what I should do," she whispered, hoping for an answer to her question.

The next few weeks she met Ramona down at the spring, but she did her best to keep away from Jessie. And for the first time in her life, she didn't tell Ramona about her hidden feelings for Jessie. Maybe if she didn't think or talk about them, they'd go away.

CHAPTER 6

Hudson

It was August the twenty-fourth the summer vacation from school was ending and a new school year would be starting right after Labor Day.

Charlie opened the screen door, holding it with her foot not letting it slam, as she stepped out onto the verandah. She walked over to Joshua and her daddy and set down two glasses of cold, sweet ice tea on a table between them.

"Thank you Charlie," they both said smiling at her. She leaned back in the swing gently pushing it with her toes looking at the two men's troubled faces.

"Joshua, we shor' need the rain but a full blown hurricane isn't what we need, not right now," Everett announced. "That Hurricane Cleo is growing in the Atlantic and it's been a while since we've had one around these parts."

"No sir, it doesn't look good Everett, but the crops are a loss anyways, and I figure there's not much we can do about Mother Nature. I guess we'll have to try again next year," Joshua answered.

"Well, we need to keep up with this storm. It's coming right up the coast and this could be a crackerjack of a storm. I reckon we'd better get some supplies together and check the shutters on the house, the one upstairs to the right is loose," Everett added grabbing squeezing his hands on the arm of the rocker.

"Well, I'll go into town tomorrow and get some more kerosene. The lamps in the living room are getting low," Joshua said leaning back in the rocker.

"Daddy, can I go down to the spring and swim, it's so hot and stuffy?" Charlie asked stopping the swing with her toes.

"Not alone, Charlie, you don't get in that water alone young lady and you keep watch around you."

"I won't, I promise, and Ramona maybe there," she answered leaning over giving her daddy a hug as she smiled up at Joshua.

"Now you don't stay to long down there, your mother might need your help in the kitchen."

"I'll be back in time to help her with supper," Charlie yelled to her father running down the dirt path she'd made over the summer, feeling the crunchy, crispy grass under her feet.

She stopped running. Charlie heard moans of a struggle. She dashed down her path her heart beating fast afraid it was going to jump out of her chest. She slid to a stop.

There in front of her was Jessie wrestling with Hudson across the creek, the two thrashing about rolling on the ground, fiercely fighting.

Hudson slid a knife from his belt swishing it in the air. He then gripped the knife thrusting it with all his strength stabbing at Jessie's chest. She gasped. Jessie flung his arm blocking the attack, but the knife sliced his arm open. Blood gushed, dripping onto the ground.

Charlie's air was sucked from her lungs.

Lying on the bank was Ramona. She wasn't moving her face buried down into the dirt. Charlie let out a blood-curdling scream. She raced across the rock dam to Ramona. She slid next to

Ramona's limp body lifting her swollen face up in her hand. Ramona took in a breath and Charlie did a sigh of relief.

She gently laid Ramona's head on the ground. Her eyes were on fire remembering the creep touching her and even more terrified of what he'd done to Ramona.

She pulled her pistol out of its holster holding it tight with both hands.

She looked up seeing Jessie was continuing to struggle with the slimy animal, Hudson.

Jessie peered up and saw what she was doing. He shook his head yes. He knocked Hudson down to the ground. Hudson started to stand up, but before he could move. Charlie didn't hesitate this time and pulled the trigger knocking her body against the ground.

Blood ran down the vile man's chest his terrified eyes looked at her. "You bitch, I knew you were trouble ever since that one day," he shouted in a gurgling voice. He lifted his hands up in the air with his fingers dripping in blood clawing at her. He let out a moan and fell back to the ground his cold eyes stared at Charlie, and then – he didn't move.

"Charlie," Everett yelled running down the path with Joshua right behind him. "Are you alright."

Jessie jumped up and ran to Ramona. She whimpered and looked up at her brother with fear in her eyes seeing blood gushing down his arm.

Joshua raced after Jessie. He untied his bandana from around his neck and tightly wrapped it around Jessie's arm.

Everett squatted down next to Charlie who was still sitting on the ground staring at Hudson. He grabbed her pistol out of her hand. She didn't move or speak. She just stared at the man she'd just killed.

Her eyes peered over at Jessie, his head tilted nodding yes, and he winked, telling her she did a good job. She'd saved his and Ramona's life. Jessie pulled his shirt off seeing Ramona's torn top and squatted near wrapping the bloody shirt around Ramona's trembling body.

"Ramona, are you alright?" questioned Everett.

A piercing scream came from behind Ramona and Jessie. Jack and Grace Ledford stood seeing their children next to Hudson's bloody body.

Jack hurried to Jessie fearing the worst as he stared down at his daughter.

"Ramona," Grace cried, "Ohhhhhhh, Jessie." She looked up at Jessie her fingers gently touched the bandana. His arm covered in and dripping in blood.

"Mom," Ramona cried out, "all I remember is sitting here by the spring. I heard someone coming up behind me. I thought it was Jessie, but it was him," she sobbed. Her terrified eyes looked at the disgusting man covered in blood. "He grabbed me and put his hand over my mouth and knocked me down to the ground. He began clawing at me, tearing at my top. I kicked him, but he just laughed pulling his body over me. His one hand wrapped around my body covering my mouth. His other hand was all over my body, as he grinned at me. I fought him and the last thing I remembered was seeing his fist coming at me, until Charlie was looking down on me." She looked at Charlie a questioning look on her face.

Jessie bent down grabbing his sister with his right arm letting his left arm hang by his side dripping in blood. "He didn't hurt you. I walked up when he punch you and I kicked the bastard in the side knocking him off of you. He won't hurt anyone ever again," said Jessie looking over at Charlie.

"I'll get the sheriff," said Joshua hurrying up the path to Bella Oak.

"Come on, let's get all of you to the house," Everett declared, helping Charlie from the ground.

"I have to see to the youngins back at the house," Grace answered worriedly, holding onto Ramona.

"You go see to them Mom. I will be fine I have Jessie and Charlie," Ramona assured standing up by Charlie with blood oozing from her swollen lip.

"Jessie, your arm, it needs seeing to," Grace said trembling.

"Pearl will see to him, he'll be fine," Everett responded. "Come on Jack let's get them back to the house, and then Jack, you and I'll see to this piece of shit."

Pearl washed the blood from Jessie's arm and put a tight bandage on. She gave Ramona small bag of ice to place on her swollen face. Martha handed Jessie one of Everett's clean shirts and then she helped Ramona slip on one of Charlie's clean tops.

"Well, I guess I was wrong, Charlie," said Martha looking over at her daughter, "you did good saving Jessie and Ramona."

"Yes, you did, but I'm sorry I didn't take care of that son of bitch myself," Everett added angrily.

"Jack – Everett, Deputy Otis is here," Joshua yelled from the driveway. Jack and Everett turned and hurried to the foyer and out onto the verandah. The group of men rushed down the path to the spring creek.

Jessie, a stern look on his face, stepped out onto the verandah and wrapped his good arm around one of the porch's post squeezing it tight. Charlie softly closed the screen door moving over by him. The evening sun was glowing in the west so beautiful, but they both knew how horrible this day could've ended.

Charlie reached up caressing Jessie's good arm, remembering his tender touch when they sat in the old oak tree. Her emotions had gone wild seeing Hudson stabbing at Jessie, knowing if he hadn't blocked the knife attack, he could've been lying next to Hudson.

"Ramona is alright, you did good Jessie," Charlie whispered.

"Red, it was to close," whispered Jessie shaking his head tensing his body. "Ramona is so innocent and sweet." His fisted hand squeezed tight his head peered downward at the floor. "Thank you," he offered. His head turned from her looking down at the verandah's floor his wild blonde hair blowing in the breeze.

She reached up pushing his hair back from his eyes. "Jessie, you saved Ramona."

He reached over gently touching her shoulder their eyes meet as he pulled her close. She didn't move away from him. They both froze, each remembering their kiss. He squeezed her tight, sliding his good arm around her shoulder their bodies snuggling. They both couldn't deny their feelings anymore; fate, life was bringing them together. He held onto her not letting go and she could feel his heart beating faster and faster. She wanted to reach up and pull his face down to her. Time seemed to stand still for the two until Ramona stepped out onto the verandah letting the screen door slam. Jessie let go of his grip on Charlie.

Ramona stood on the huge veranda happily smiling staring at her best friend and her brother, not saying a word, but looks told the whole story.

The evening did end with Jessie, Ramona, and Jack walking down the path to the creek going home.

Charlie lay wide awake in her soft safe bed.

"Charlie," Everett quietly called out standing at her door, "are you awake?"

"Daddy," she called back to him.

"That's what I thought. Honey, you need some rest. You did what you needed to do. That man wouldn't have stopped until he or Jessie was dead."

"But, daddy the whole mess keeps playing over and over in my mind."

"It will for a while, but you'll be fine and I'm proud of you girl. I guess you are a true Bellamead. Now, you need some rest, and we'll talk more tomorrow."

"Thank you Daddy," she said as he bent over giving her hug.

"Goodnight, Charlie," he whispered closing the door. She lay back on her pillow seeing Jessie's eyes in her mind staring at her, not Hudson's anymore.

CHAPTER 7

Hurricane Cleo

August 26th, 1960, Friday night.

"Well…." Everett began as he sat at the supper table. "It seems the hurricane is headed our way and not altering its course. It'll be here by Sunday or maybe before and it's gonna be a whopper of a storm."

"Daddy," Charlie asked in a high voice, "it's really that big of hurricane, and it's going to be dangerous?"

"Charlie, I reckon it could be," her daddy answered. "What's wrong, Charlie; we'll be fine. Don't worry so. This is a strong old house."

"I'm not worried about us," Charlie leaned back in her chair and gulped, "but the Ledford's home isn't very strong."

"I've seen that home," agreed Joshua anxiously. "It's not much. Everett we have to do something. They need to come here and ride out the storm."

"Jack Ledford won't come and stay during the storm," Everett declared. "He's too proud."

"Everett, you go over there and convince that man to let go of his pride," Martha joined in as she picked up the dishes from the kitchen table. "This house has withstood many hurricanes and I suspect that it'll withstand many more."

"Lordy, she's right," Pearl chimed in. "We can't have those children out there when this storm hits; it just wouldn't be right."

"Alright, I'll go see what I can do in the morning," Everett said shaking his head. Everett knew he had to bring the Ledford family back with him. A smile emerged on the corner of his mouth looking over at his wife and daughter who always got their way.

The next morning Charlie ran outside and stood on the verandah. She saw her daddy walking toward the spring on her worn path.

"Daddy, wait," she called out. "Can I go with you over to the Ledfords and see Ramona?" she questioned walking along side of him.

"No, you stay here and I'll be right back. I need to talk to Jack alone," he answered stepping onto the rocks of her dam. He stopped. "Girl, you shor' have been busy down here," he said moving his head back and forth and looking into the pool of water Charlie had dammed up with the large rocks.

Charlie tightened her mouth and held her breath, wondering what he was going to say about her rock dam.

"The water should flow over the rocks without any problems even in a flood," he added, "so it can stay." He smiled shaking his head proud of her initiative on damming up the creek.

She breathed a sigh of relief and sat down in the cool grass by the spring looking at her reflection in the water. Even the spring was slowing down and its water wasn't flowing very fast since it was so dry and hot. She couldn't concentrate for hoping her daddy could convince Mr. Ledford to come stay at the plantation during the storm and she promised herself to stay away from Jessie. She heard her dad coming back along the path from the Ledford's place.

"C'mon Charlie," Everett announced proudly stepping on the rocks of the dam crossing the creek. "We have a lot of work ahead of us; they'll be over later this afternoon."

She grabbed hold of her daddy squeezing him, as he puffed up with pride. "I knew you could do it. Just like Joshua says you could talk a dog out of bone if you wanted," she proclaimed letting go of her daddy and running up the hill to Bella Oak.

She made it to the kitchen door before her daddy and hurried into the kitchen. "Mom, the Ledford's will be coming later this afternoon! Daddy did it!"

"I knew he could convince them. Now, we've got a lot of work to do. Charlene, you go, and get the guest bedrooms clean and get some extra towels out of the hall closet. We'll be able to sleep upstairs at least for a while."

"Martha, I guessed you heard?" Everett said softly closing the kitchen screen door.

"Yes, and I am relieved," she admitted carrying a basket of wet clothes walking past him going out the screen door to hang out her last load of clothes.

"Well Charlie, there is one thing," her daddy began in a quiet voice. "Jessie isn't coming over here tonight. He's staying at the farm to see to a cow that is about to deliver a calf."

"Daddy, the storm might hit tonight," snapped Charlie.

"I know, but Jack wouldn't leave the cow alone. That cow has had trouble in the past. He had to sell some of his herd to live this summer and desperately needs this cow and calf. It's too late to try and move her to our barn."

"That ole barn out back of their house…it's not much."

"I know, but it's the only way Jack would come over here and Jessie knows how important that calf is to them. As soon as the calf is born, he's going to come here. He's a very resourceful young man and he'll be fine. Now…" said Everett taking a breath staring down at his daughter. "Young lady what is going on with

Jessie and you? I see the same look in your bright green eyes your mom had twenty years ago, a look I'll never forget."

"Jessie is just a friend and nothing else, Daddy," she answered knowing that was only half of the truth.

"Well – he'll be safe, I promise," her daddy assured putting his arm around her. He grinned, knowing there was more than friendship between the two. "I won't let anything happen to that boy." "Thank you Daddy," she said hugging him back smelling the scent of Old Spice. "I better get to work cleaning the upstairs guest bedrooms or mom'll be upset."

"We don't need her upset. I'll go see what Joshua is doing. Stop worrying, Charlie."

He turned and went outside and she hurried up the long staircase to the guest bedrooms to prepare, but her mind kept thinking about Jessie sitting in that old rickety barn with the pregnant cow.

Charlie and Martha scooted tables out of the way making room for everyone in the living room and they cooked a large pot of beef stew to feed the Ledford's crew. Pearl was busy at her small house out back, cleaning and putting things away and packing to stay in the plantation home for the next few days. Things were buzzing around the old home as it was once more being prepared as a storm shelter, just as it had been in the past.

"Alright, young lady," Martha said as she began washing up the dishes in the sink. "Your daddy said you were extra worried about Jessie. Is there something we need to talk about?"

"No ma'am."

"Honey," she declared, swishing the dishes in the sink, "Jessie is a nice young man, but you and he come from different backgrounds. It jus' wouldn't be right for you two," she added dipping the dishes into hot water and then sliding them into the drain board to dry.

"Mom, Jessie isn't like that and Jeffery just wants Bella Oak, not me anyways."

"Now Charlene, you can't jus' let any sweet talking boy get to you," she snapped turning back around looking at Charlie. "If you were to marry Jessie, you'd always worry that he married you for your money."

"I've told you; I'm not marrying anyone from around here."

"Well, Jeffery does care about you and he doesn't need the money, and yes, he cares about Bella Oak too. Honey, you better be careful. Young lady your eyes are telling a different story about Jessie."

"Well…I just have a strange feeling that something bad is going to happen to Jessie, a feeling that I don't like."

"Oh, so you're like your daddy now," her mom said shaking her head. "Well, that ain't good 'cause your father's feelings are usually correct." Martha shook out the dishtowel hanging it on the stoves handle. "We'll keep an eye on Jessie," she assured walking over putting her arm around Charlie, squeezing her tight. "Honey, I jus' want the best for you, but you need to stay away from Jessie while they're here and not give into those feelings."

Charlie looked at her mom… thinking of Jessie.

"Oh, they must be here, I hear a lot of noise out front," Martha called out hurrying to the front door.

Charlie walked out onto the verandah and a crew of blonde haired kids piled out of the back of the old truck. Grace Ledford had the baby in her arms and walked up the steps to Charlie handing the baby to her. Charlie gasped; she'd never held a baby before and didn't know what to do.

"That's not how to hold her," came a voice to her delight as she spun around. "Here, hold her tight," said Jessie taking her arms and wrapping them tighter around the baby. "She won't bite, not yet. She doesn't have many teeth," Jessie said, laughing.

"Jessie, I thought you had to stay at the barn?" she asked happily.

"I do, Poppa is there now and wanted me to drive Momma over here and help her with the little ones. I'll take his place when I get them settled. Red, thanks for sending your dad over to convince them to come here." His head ducked to the porch's floor as he shifted his feet. "This could've been horrible if we'd stayed in that old house of ours."

"Jessie?" she took a deep breath. "I don't want you to go back to that barn. I have – a bad feeling."

"Hey, Red I'll be fine, some peace and quiet. Just wait, you'll be wanting to change places with me after a while, with this bunch to tend to," he said. His hand softly squeezed her arm. "I'll see you later, I promise," he said jumping down the steps to unload the truck.

"Hey, Debbie seems to like you; she doesn't go to many people," Ramona assured standing looking at Charlie holding the baby.

Charlie didn't say anything; she just stood and watched Jessie unload the truck.

"Charlie, I'm worried too," said Ramona, "but there isn't anything we can do, he'll be okay."

Charlie looked down at the blonde hair, blue-eyed baby that was looking up at her. "I hope so," she whispered as her voice trailed off.

Mrs. Ledford came over with a big smile on her face. "Debbie shor' is content with you Charlie. Here, it's time for her nap," she said taking the baby from Charlie's arms. "Thank you for holding her."

"Come with me Grace, I'll show you where she can sleep for her nap; we set up Charlene's old baby bed upstairs in one of the guest bedrooms. Honey, you look tired. Why don't you take a nap with her?" Pearl insisted.

"Oh, I couldn't do that. I have the boys to look after and I'm shor' there is plenty of work for me to do before the storm comes," Grace answered following Pearl up the stairs.

"The boys will be fine and we have everything under control. Plus, we have Charlene and Ramona. You jus' rest for awhile, it is going to be a long couple of days."

"The clouds are racing by." Charlie peered out the window anxiously settling in on the window seat in her bedroom.

"Well…are you going to talk and tell me what's going on with Jessie or do I have to drag it out of you?" Ramona asked excitedly.

"Okay, I can't keep a secret from you, Yes, I confess, I like Jessie. Are you happy now?" said Charlie turning from the window staring over at Ramona.

"Yes," Ramona squealed, falling onto the bed. "Finally, I knew he has liked you for years, but I promised I wouldn't say anything, but you wouldn't have believed me anyways. It took you long enough to figure it out."

"It doesn't change my plans," Charlie said sitting down on the bed by her friend. "I'm still moving away and not living here --- Ramona, stop smiling so much."

"We'll see what the future holds for you," Ramona giggled and her blues eyes sparkled, dreaming of Charlie and Jessie. "Oh, that is Debbie crying. I'll go and get her," said Ramona jumping off the bed running to the bedroom door.

"Good, I was saved by the baby," Charlie called out to Ramona as she hurried out the door.

Ramona walked back into the room with the baby in her arms. "Momma is still sleeping and I didn't want to wake her. On the other hand, Debbie is hungry. First though, she's wet and I need to change her." She laid a clean cloth diaper on the bed laying Debbie on the bed next to Charlie.

"Not on my bed," groaned Charlie.

"Oh, stop I'll put a towel under her. Here watch her, so I can get one from the bathroom."

Charlie leaned over by the content baby with drool running down her chin. "Babies are messy and stinky, aren't they?"

"Yes," said Ramona laughing pulling the plastic pants and the wet cloth diaper off. She quickly secured the dry diaper with wide pink pens.

"Alright, now you get to see how messy babies really are. It's feeding time."

"Pearl," said Ramona, hurrying into the kitchen. "Debbie is hungry and I don't know where Momma put her food. I guess I need to wake her."

"No, don't wake ya momma, let her sleep, she is just plain wore out. I have some mashed potatoes and applesauce in the refrigerator. Let me warm up the potatoes and I'll see to the baby.

Ramona sat Debbie in the highchair. "Pearl, do you need some help?"

"No, sweetie, I've fed many babies in my time," she assured scooting a chair up next to the high chair.

"Mom, what do you need us to do?" asked Charlie.

Martha looked at her daughter. "Charlene, you and Ramona get the table set in the dining room and move some pillows from the living room for the boys to sit on in two of the chairs. I also need you to bring in the last load of clothes. They are getting twisted on the lines and I'm sure they're dry in this heat."

"Mom," Charlie asked lifting the large bowls from the cabinet, "where's the storm?"

"It'll be moving on shore in a few hours and we'll be getting the feeder bands with heavy rain before then."

"Did you see your daddy and Joshua?"

"I don't know where Everett is, but Joshua is helping Jack secure the Ledford's barn," Peal answered cleaning Debbie's face with a washcloth.

"Well, I was going to send one of them to the barn with some food for Jessie. Would you two like to take him some stew and cornbread when you get done?"

"Sure, get his food ready. This won't take us long," added Charlie, excitedly, as she pulled out the silverware from the china cabinet drawer.

"I'll get the clothes off the line and you set the table Charlie, then we can get done faster," offered Ramona pushing open the screen door.

"Oh, everyone is busy," called out Grace walking into the kitchen, "I'm so sorry that I slept so long. Ramona, you should have woke me, I didn't need to sleep that long."

"Yes, you did. You were tired, and with that houseful, I know why. Now sit down; we are doing fine and Pearl is enjoying rocking the baby on the front porch. It's been a while since we had one around here. I have the beef stew and cornbread ready and the girls are seeing to everything else. Here is a nice glass of ice tea. Grace, we better enjoy something cold to drink before we lose electricity," said Martha shaking her head worriedly.

"Alright Mom, we're done and Ramona set the basket of clean clothes back on the washer. Do you have Jessie's food ready?"

"Yep, here," Martha said handing Charlie the basket. "Now, you two don't stay to long. That sky's getting dark."

"We want," called out Charlie stepping out the back door with Ramona following her along the path to Rock Creek.

Ramona took off running past her leading the way to the barn. Joshua was busily finishing up nailing a few more boards on the side of the barn. Charlie moaned staring up at the old boards. Joshua was correct it wasn't any better than the house and that terrified her.

"Alright, food!" Jessie yelled out the door. "Charlie, stop frowning and," he added waving his hand, "c'mon inside."

"How's she doing?" questioned Ramona, squatting down by the cow softly rubbing the cow's head. "I hope nothing happens to that calf or the cow. Poppa said we really need them both."

"So far things are fine and I'm betting the closer the storm gets, she'll deliver and then this'll be over. Now, what did you bring? All right, beef stew. Oh, that smells good and warm buttered cornbread. Great, some iced tea. It's so hot in here, that tea'll cool me off a little. And even some fried pies! Well, at least I'll go happy."

Charlie hit him. "Don't say things like that."

"Red, I'll be alright. Joshua is fixing the barn, and I'll be fine. Sorry, I didn't mean to upset you."

"I don't want to hear that kind of talk, either," said Ramona standing up from the cow, and then poking her brother with her index finger.

"Girls, we need to get back to the house," called Joshua stepping inside the barn.

"Okay," Ramona hollered.

"Here's a battery radio, Jessie," Joshua exclaimed, setting the radio in the corner of the stall. "So you can keep up with the storm. Now if it gets to bad get to the plantation and don't worry about the cow. Cows have been having calves on their own for years. Jessie, I mean it; don't take no chances."

"I won't Joshua, and I'll see you later," Jessie assured, leaning over hugging Ramona, then he turned and pulled Charlie close holding her tight against him. He leaned down still holding onto her gently kissing her on the forehead. He didn't move for a second looking into her green eyes brimming with tears. He gave her the smile that everything would be all right, as she reached up touching his face brushing his wild hair from his eyes.

The girls followed Joshua back to the house and Mr. Ledford pulled up in his truck. "Jack let's put your truck in the barn," shouted Joshua hurrying over to the truck.

The first rain began to fall and the sky was becoming dark as night as fierce clouds raced in the sky.

Charlie stood on the verandah looking out past the creek seeing the old twisted live oak sitting up on the hill blowing in the breeze. "That tree is our special tree, Jessie," she thought to herself.

Her daddy walked outside. "Time to eat," he said putting his arm around Charlie leading her into the house.

The twins sat on their pillows in the dining room chairs slurping the stew. Charlie pulled her chair out and sat down, but couldn't eat very much. She sat quietly listening to everyone as they discussed the hurricane. She was glad when the supper was over and she quickly began picking up the bowls and clearing off the table.

"That was great stew, Martha, and the cornbread was delicious, thank you," Jack said kindly, scooting his chair back away from the table.

"Pearl, I can wash the dishes if you'll hold Debbie," offered Grace picking up Debbie out of her highchair.

"I'd be glad to hold Debbie, but you come with me and sit in the living room. The girls can clean the kitchen. I think they need to stay busy," Pearl offered looking over at Charlie. Pearl could see how worried she was about Jessie, making the old woman smile inside. She knew Jessie was perfect for Charlie, not Jeffery.

Ramona began humming as she washed the dishes, a chore she did each night, and Charlie dried and put each dish away. "Listen to that wind. It's like a sad animal howling," Ramona's voice rose uneasily.

Charlie nodded. "It's hot in here. Let's go outside on the verandah and sit," she said overwhelmed hanging up the dishtowel on the stove's handle. "Daddy, can we sit out on the verandah for a little while?" Charlie asked walking into the living room.

"Sure honey, but there ain't any chairs,"

"That's alright," said Charlie pushing open the old wooden screen door. She went to the side of the porch and sat down on the old plank floor. The light was fading from the sky and the strong feeder bands from the storm were moving in a lot sooner than expected. Ramona joined her, but neither girl said anything. They just watched the sky and watched the path to the creek hoping to see Jessie coming to Bella Oaks.

CHAPTER 8

Jessie

"Charlie, the wind is getting too strong. We need to go inside," pleaded Ramona.

Charlie nodded her head yes, but didn't move.

Ramona leaned over and pulled on her arm. "Staying out here ain't going to help him."

"Daddy, where is the storm?" Charlie called out in a quavering voice as she slid down on the floor in the living room. She shivered listening to the breeze whistle a mournful cry from the one open window in the living room.

"Hurricane Cleo is coming ashore on the north side of Savannah and is heading this way with winds of one hundred and fifty five miles an hour and she's not letting up. This is going to be a doozy of a storm and a long night and that wind is shor' getting fierce." Everett commented as he leaned over in his chair, worriedly wringing his hands together as they all listened to the radio.

Bam!

"What in tarnation was that?" yelled Everett leaning back in his chair.

Joshua jumped from his chair and looked out the front door.

"One of the old oak limbs has hit the roof of the verandah," he hollered shaking his head, mumbling, "not good."

Grace grabbed the boys bringing them close as the lights blinked and darkness fell over the room with only the light coming from the lightning quickly flashing every few minutes.

"Gosh durn it…there goes the electric for a few days," cried out Joshua grabbing the matches from his shirt pocket. He struck a match with the smell of sulfur floating in the room. He lifted the tall glass from one the kerosene lamps, lighting it and going around the room lighting the rest of the lamps. "I shor' didn't think the electric would go out this fast."

"Those feeder bands are getting way too strong, I'm going after Jessie," Jack Ledford called out frantically standing from his chair. "This isn't good if the storm is coming right over us. I can't leave that boy out there in that old barn all alone, it's just too dangerous."

"Here," declared Everett, throwing a rain jacket at Jack. "I'm going with you." He leaned over kissing Martha and patting Charlie on the head. "We'll all be fine, remember I promised," he said slipping his jacket on grabbing two flashlights from the mantle.

"Look….Charlie," Jack paused leaning over by her. "I'd never put my son's life ahead of the calves. I was hoping the storm'd go on up the coast and not come in directly over us."

"Come on Jack, we need to get the boy to safety," Everett called out. He turned the doorknob and the wind shoved the door wide open. The cool air blew into the room.

Charlie and Ramona sat watching out the open window, now worrying about both of their dads and Jessie. The women were quiet and the only noise in the room was Debbie cooing. The thunder boomed and rumbled shaking the old house as the lightning lit up the outside blinking brightly inside the living room for a second at a time. The smell of smoke from the kerosene lamps filled the room with the small light flickering, hitting the solemn faces. The wind howled sending chills down Charlie's spine. A loud crash made her jump up and raced to the dining room window.

"The barn door was just blown off!" she screamed. "The storm is ripping it apart!"

The twins began crying with terror in their small faces as Grace hugged them even tighter. Pearl cuddled the baby in her large arms not letting anything get close. Martha was rocking viciously in the rocker as if it might help somehow. Joshua sat leaning over with his hands laced together looking down at the floor. The storm was coming in with a vengeance. He knew the warm waters in the Atlantic mixing with the dry air would make the storm mad as it moved closer to them.

Time advanced on slowly as they sat waiting anxiously for the men to come back. The bong of the old grandfather clock in the foyer made Grace jump. Charlie watched the slow tick of the pendulum while the winds picked up speed. The old home moaned as limbs pounded the side of the house. They heard crashing from some glass breaking upstairs when a limb shot like a bullet through the shutters crashing through the windows. Charlie vigilantly sat watching out the front window.

"I see some flashlights," Ramona yelled. "They're coming, all three of them. I can see them when the lightning brightens up the outside …Oh no, Jessie's hurt."

Charlie swiftly pulled the large wooden front door open wide. Joshua grabbed hold of the screen door. Blood was pouring off Jessie's lifeless face and dripping onto the floor as the two men held onto him dragging him into the living room. Grace screamed. Joshua grabbed hold of Jessie and helped to lay him on the sofa.

Pearl handed Debbie to Ramona and grabbed a handful of rags. Blood ran down Jessie's face and the rags were quickly saturated. Charlie stood to the side shivering with fear and staring at all of the red. A long deep cut was on the side of Jessie's head right above his right eye. Pearl worked feverishly trying to get the bleeding stopped using her large hands to put pressure on the gash.

"Pearl, what do we do?" cried Grace kneeling down by her son. "The blood isn't stopping and he's losing way too much!"

"Here, you just keep putting pressure on the cut and it'll stop!"

"I don't know?" Grace spoke with her voice trembling. "There's so much blood."

"Alright, there," Pearl announced, "the bleeding is slowing down. Now, we have to get a tight bandage on the cut, if we squeeze the cut together it should be all right. You know that cut really could use some stitches." Her head shook back and forth. "But, we can't get him to the hospital."

"Keep squeezing Pearl and I'll put the tape and bandage on," Grace shouted franticly.

"Well, that's all we can do," Pearl sighed wiping her brow with her sleeve of her dress.

Jessie lay still, unconscious on the sofa taking in shallow breaths. Charlie sat on the floor next to her mother's chair not taking her eyes off of him. Her body trembled looking at the red soaked rags lying in the pan on the floor. The group sat anxiously very quietly, knowing he needed to wake up soon to be sure he was alright.

"Oh, Pearl," whispered Grace in a quivering voice leaning over next to Pearl. "This isn't good. That cut is deep and right above his eye. You know what this could do, don't you?" she said overwhelmed. She sat there softly rubbing her son's arm in a nervous constant motion.

"I know," Pearl whispered back. "We just have to pray he'll be fine and God doesn't let him lose his sight, but first he has to wake up. Then, we'll worry about his eye."

"I can't lose my son," Grace sniffed. "He really needed to go the hospital, but I guess we did all we could."

"Sweetie, he's in God's hands now," offered Pearl sitting down in her rocker.

Charlie gasped! No…not his eyesight! Jessie had to wake up and be all right. She couldn't lose him.

She whispered, "Jessie…please, wake up." Charlie could see in the low light of the oil lamp that the swelling and blue colors appearing on his face. Her mind wouldn't let go of what Pearl said, remembering the sketch she'd seen. Losing his eyesight would devastate him. Drawing was his life. She kept whispering very quietly,

"Please, wake up, Jessie. Please, God, let him wake up and be okay." She then leaned over near him, so no one could hear. "Jessie….I love you, please wake up," she whispered wiping away her tears so no one would notice.

The old clock kept ticking with Martha feverously rocking back and forth. The storm wasn't letting up and hours passed by slowly with the roar of the storm growing along with the tension in the room.

Suddenly…Jessie moaned and his eyes blinked looking up at everyone. "Mom, we have twin calves," he announced looking over at his mom with his blue eyes staring right at her.

Even the room seemed to sigh with relief, and Grace leaned over by him, kissed her son on the cheek, and softly rubbed his arm.

"Some boards from the roof fell and hit him on the head," Everett explained. "We found him lying on the floor unconscious. It was a good thing we went to get him." The man stepped over by Jessie, looking down on the boy.

"Grace," said Jack taking a moment, catching his breath. "One side of the roof over by the kitchen has been blown off the house." The man with the wild blonde hair, who looked just like Jessie, bowed his shaking head. "It's a good thing we weren't there with the children."

"Oh…Jessie your room and all of your drawings," Ramona frantically cried out!

"That's alright, I'll draw more," added Jessie sadly looking up at everyone. His eyes and tired bruised face looked over at Charlie.

"That you won't have to worry about," announced Grace proudly. "I brought all of your drawings with me. They're safe for now, right here," she said smiling down at her son.

"Well, Red, I guess you were right about your feelings. This hasn't been an easy storm," Jessie admitted as he looked at her with exhausted eyes. "I guess next time, I should listen to you." He reached his arm out to her.

She took his hand in hers scooting close, as he caressed her hand in front of everyone, not worrying what her mom thought. Everett and Pearl smiled proudly. Charlie lightly stroked his hand. "Thank you, God," she whispered with Jessie still smiling at her.

"Now, you jus' rest and you'll be okay," Pearl chuckled, "I couldn't lose my biggest fried pie fan." The big woman laughed with her large body shaking, finally relaxing as she leaned back in her rocker.

Everett closed the last window on the verandah and the shutter making the room stuffy. Everyone found a place to sit and listened to the cry of the storm. Hurricane Cleo wasn't giving up easy, with the torrential rains coming down as the feeder bands whirled around the home. They could hear trees falling and debris hitting the side of the old house, but the plantation home stood strong.

CHAPTER 9

Will You Still Love Me Tomorrow

Charlie scooted next to the back wall by Ramona. Everyone was safe. She finally fell asleep lying against Ramona. She woke with a start with the sun shining in through the screen door hitting her face.

"Red, I declare you wiggle a lot when you sleep. You must dream a lot," Jessie whispered, sitting in a rocker smiling down on her.

"The storm," she whispered back, "is it gone?"

"Yep, don't wake Ramona." He reached his arm over pulling her up away from Ramona. "She didn't sleep well last night either. You two worry too much about things you can't change."

Charlie stood and he pulled her close. "Let's go out on the verandah and sit." He lead her out the screen door and over to the side of the verandah. He reached up and untied the swing from the side rail, letting it fall down.

"Happy Birthday, Red," he said pushing the swing back with his legs gently as he looked down at the floor. "Sorry, I don't have a present for you. At least you can get your driver's license now and can quit driving everywhere without one," he teased.

"Your being alright is the best present I could have this birthday," she said sliding over next to him. She wasn't hiding her feelings or holding back, not worrying that it was August the twenty-ninth, her birthday.

"Well, Miss Charlene Olivia Bellamead, you're sixteen, not a kid anymore. I guess you're a true Southern belle, a real lady now."

"A Southern belle," she laughed, "maybe you did hit your head harder than we thought."

He leaned back against the swing smiling with more thoughts swirling in his head.

"How's your head feeling? That's some cut you have. You lost a lot of blood and your face sure is bruised." She leaned over still looking into his clear blue eyes, remembering what the two women had said about his eyesight.

"I'm fine now, my head hurts some, but I did get a lot of blood on your mom's rug. I hope it'll come clean."

"Mom won't fret about that old rug. Oh….I wonder how the dam did. Do you feel up to a walk down to the spring?"

"Only if you'll help me?" He tilted his head to the side grinning. He stopped the swing with his long legs and stood up. He reached his hand out to her.

"You were moving just fine a few minutes ago," she said grinning back taking his hand. She wrapped her arm around him and he grabbed her tight.

"My pain comes and goes," he whispered, "and I might get dizzy."

"If you do get dizzy, then I might have to push you in the water. Spring water cures all."

They walked down the steps of the large verandah out into the fresh air with the wind lightly blowing. She held onto Jessie, carefully stepping over all the limbs and debris lying on the ground.

"Everything smells so clean and new," said Charlie letting go of Jessie, twirling around in a circle. She looked up at the trees dripping down on them with fresh droplets.

"Yes, it does."

"Wow! Look at the water flowing. Everything is back to normal. I knew it would work. It did take some dirt on the sides of the bank, but the dam held and didn't flood," she said excitedly.

"Come on over here and sit down," Jessie called out to her, leaning back on the bank of the creek in the wet grass.

She could see he was still weak and trying not to show how drained he was. Even the walk from the house had worn him out.

"We won't get to sit out here much more since school is starting next week," he reminded her.

She sat down by him, feeling the dampness of the grass on her shorts, knowing she was getting way too close. Not good, she could feel her emotions taking over, remembering what her mom had warned. "This is your senior year and you'll be able to leave this place next summer." She looked into his blue eyes waiting for a reaction. "I still have another year to get away."

"I have to keep my grades up to try and get a scholarship. I first need to find a job to make some money or I want be able to leave," he assured.

She sat quiet for a second thinking about him staying next year and not leaving. Secretly, she was hoping he wouldn't leave. "Mr. Kent said you could get a scholarship for art if you want. Maybe that would work for you."

"Something will work," he said, not worrying like always. "Oh it is so nice out here." He leaned back on his elbows, peering over at her.

"Well, I'm glad your mom saved your drawings and I hope someday to get to see some of them." She turned over lying flat on her stomach with the wetness of the grass soaking her top with her head in her hands studying him. He lay on the ground looking up at the sky.

He could feel her eyes were on him as his body heated, knowing he had to be cautious. He had years of hidden passion building inside of him. He had loved her for his entire life. Now, she was lying next to him and this was more than his emotions could handle. This was a dream that he had dreamt of each night, but he knew this wasn't right, knowing they were from two different worlds: him so poor and her, a daughter of a wealthy plantation owner. He rolled over on his side not leaving or worrying with his face turned toward her.

"Maybe…someday, I'll show my drawings to you," he offered, finally answering her question trying to bring himself back from his dream.

Her eyes studied him now dreaming her own dream of him holding her, questioning in her mind what it would feel like to be that close to him. She was surprised at her thoughts, never imagining her emotions would be this strong. He grinned at her and she wondered if he knew what she was thinking and if her face might be turning red, feeling her face flush, quickly turning her face from him.

He couldn't stop himself. He reached over turning her face back around, pulling her close with their lips meeting again. He touched her hair with his soft hand caressing her neck and he pulled their bodies together. His holding her tight was as wonderful as she had dreamed, and she did not want to move away. He pulled her body over with his hand gently gliding down her side, as she reached up wrapping her arms around him.

She squeezed her eyes closed with her hands becoming her eyes. She felt his arms with his muscles tighten gripping her as he rolled over. Her body was warm with sensations overtaking her mind. This was more than she could handle, but now her body was in a struggle of emotions going on between her body and her mind.

She opened her eyes seeing those blue eyes looking at her knowing the answer for both of them.

She jerked, pulling back from him quickly jumping up. "I better get back to the house, Mom and Pearl will be looking for me. I'm sure there's a lot of work to get done today." She straightened up her top and shorts, trying to get her composure back.

Jessie leaned his head back laughing, knowing she was getting away from him and not letting her emotions take over. "I'm going to stay right here for a while," he said lying back against the wet ground watching her every move. He knew this wasn't the last time the two would be together.

"If anyone needs me, you can tell them I'm down here."

"I'm sure they'll let you take some time off, but I'll let them know you're alright. It is a beautiful day." She sucked in a deep breath of the clean, fresh air remembering how it felt to be held so close.

"Yes, it is," he agreed staring at her. "Happy birthday, Red."

Charlie made it back to the house and Ramona was sitting in the swing. "Where did you go?"

"I went down to the spring to check out the dam and yes with Jessie. Don't say anything," Charlie declared with Ramona grinning as she looked at Charlie's wet clothes.

"Happy Birthday, Charlie," Ramona added, "I guess this isn't much of a birthday for you this year."

"No, you're wrong this is the best birthday ever. Everyone is safe and alright from the storm," she added.

"Yep, especially Jessie, right," Ramona added still grinning. "That was some scare last night. Now, we have some work to do. Poppa is already working on our roof with Joshua. They're putting a tarp over the roof, but it seems that we'll be staying here at least one more night," she said leaning back in the swing. "Oh, the day is so much cooler and so crisp. At least your birthday is a gorgeous day."

"Yes, it is," Charlie agreed, leaning back in the swing thinking of the kiss and Jessie holding her. "The spring also survived better than I thought. The dam worked perfect." She knew Jessie would be close for a few days, but he was safe and that was all that counted. She never wanted to feel the pain she felt watching him lie there on the sofa, so lifeless waiting for him to wake up.

"Your dad has gone to check out the outer barns and let the animals out, but your house looks fine except the big limb that fell on the roof of the verandah. A couple of windows upstairs were broken." Ramona leaned back in the swing getting comfortable pulling her legs up.

"Charlie, Ramona," came a call from inside the house.

"Yes, Momma," yelled Ramona, "we're out here swinging."

"Oh, there you are, I'm going over to the house with Martha, and Pearl is watching the little ones so I need you two to help her around the house. Happy birthday, Charlie. Sorry we've interrupted your party this year. Where's Jessie?" Grace asked.

"He's down by the spring, probably asleep. He was tired, Mrs. Ledford." Charlie explained.

"Good, he needs some rest."

"Hi Mom," Charlie called out, as Martha stepped outside onto the verandah.

"Good morning, Charlene. Oh, isn't it nice out; everything is always so sparkling after a storm." She leaned over kissing her daughter. "Happy birthday, honey. We'll have a late birthday party next week for you if that's alright. Now, we'll be back later."

"You two help Pearl," both women said in unison, walking to the truck.

We will," Ramona called back to them stopping the swing as they watched the truck back out of the driveway.

That evening the lights began to blink as they all sat at the dining room table.

"Wow, the electric's back on. That was fast," Joshua said shocked, looking over at Everett across the dining room table.

Everett started laughing. "Well, I heard a line was down by Montgomery's plantation. The electric company didn't want to hear from Zach about the electricity being out, and so they did a quick fix. Those Montgomerys do get their way most of the time. Since we are on the same line as them, we've got lights again."

Charlie could feel Jessie's eyes staring at her, as her father talked about the Montgomerys getting their way and knowing what he was thinking. Jeffery was like his father, even bullying to get his way.

"Jessie," Martha asked, "that had to be terrifying last night when the roof caved in."

"Yes'm, it was. I was finished with the calves getting them and the cow settled and was about to leave the old barn. The roof started moaning. I heard a loud cracking noise, looked up, and saw half of the roof as it flew up into the air. I tried to get to the door, but couldn't get out of the way quick enough. I pulled my arms up to cover my head, but I guess I didn't do a good job. The last thing I remembered was falling to the ground feeling the cold rain coming in soaking me, until I woke up here in the living room." He leaned up on the table and Charlie could see burses appearing on his arms.

Reaching over gently touching her son's arm, Grace shook her head and her body shuddered listening to the story.

"Happy Birthday, Charlie," Pearl sang out, walking into the dining room carrying a beautiful yellow cake with chocolate icing and sixteen candles. "Surprise!"

"Thank you, Pearl," Charlie beamed taking in a deep breath blowing out all of her candles, making her wish. She looked over at Jessie as he sat grinning at her.

It didn't take long to eat Pearl's cake. Ramona and Charlie washed up the dishes and then hurried upstairs to Charlie's room.

"Hey, you two," said Jessie as he curiously peeked in the slightly open door to the bedroom. "Can I come in? The twins are asleep in my room and I don't want to wake 'em."

"Come on in, Jessie," Ramona answered.

"Wow, this is a large room, Red. All the rooms in this house are huge. It is also very pink and frilly," he said looking at her, grinning.

"Jessie, look at all of the records Charlie has," said Ramona as she scooted over making room for her brother to sit down on the floor by her. "How are you feeling?"

"Ramona, stop worrying I'm okay," he smiled, trying to reassure her. "But, my head hurts some."

"Jessie, I know the room is really pink. My mom bought the bedspread in Charleston a couple of years ago. She believes it might bring out the girl in me, but it hasn't helped," said Charlie laughing. She looked down fiddling with the records, trying not to make eye contact with Jessie.

"Okay, Red, what's wrong, now?" asked Jessie with the grin still on his face. He did know her better than anyone and he knew she'd been trying to avoid him most of the evening. She didn't even sit by him at the supper table. She'd moved her plate over on the other side of the table.

"Nothing's wrong." Charlie smiled. "Okay, which song do you want me to play?" she asked trying to hide her feelings.

"Oh, how about this one, *Will You Still Love Me Tomorrow*," said Jessie in a soft voice. He handed Charlie the record, not hiding his thoughts anymore.

Charlie put the record on the record player. She took in a deep breath as the record began to play.

She sat listening to the words, but she couldn't help herself, turning her eyes to Jessie. She kept remembering the kiss and lying so close to him down at the creek. She sat dreaming wanting him to hold onto to her again, just as he did this morning, as the words to the song asked, "Will you love me tomorrow."

Jessie leaned back on the footboard of the bed watching Charlie, as Ramona sang along with the song. He softly sang the chorus, "Will you still love me tomorrow," as he stared into Charlie's green eyes with each chorus.

Charlie knew the answer to the song and she'd always love Jessie no matter where life took her. Her dream had changed, and the music faded into the quiet night.

CHAPTER 10

Jeffery

The next week everyone stayed busy cleaning up after the hurricane. Jack and Joshua work diligently making the repairs on the Ledford's home. Monday, September the 12th did arrive and Charlie, Ramona, and Jessie climbed on the bus to start their normal school routine. It seemed the only day for Charlie and Ramona to find time to sit at the spring was Sunday afternoons after church.

Ramona stayed busy with Chandler and each Friday night she sat in the stands watching him play football, his best cheerleader. Chandler and Ramona were making their plans for the future and her dream of living on the large plantation Whispering Pines looked like it was going to come true.

The days became weeks and October quickly arrived with the summer heat turning into cool air along with the leaves turning orange and red. Jessie began working at Jones's gas station in town to save some money for college. He wasn't backing down and he was leaving when his senior year was done, but he knew it was going to take a lot of money. He worked seven days a week. On Sunday after church, he helped Mr. Jones and worked on cars in the afternoon. Charlie only saw him on the school bus in the mornings and at church on Sunday morning, but she understood his determination to go to college next year, making his dream come true. The fall festival and county fair was imminent and Charlie did wish that Jessie would take some time off. Just one night and go with her to the carnival and hayride, but she was too stubborn to say so, and he was too stubborn to go.

"Hey, Charlie," Jeffery called out, as they walked from the lunchroom back to class. "How about going with me to the county festival and hay ride?"

"I wasn't planning on going," responded Charlie looking at Jeffery who was very unwavering. She knew that was only half of the truth. She was still waiting for Jessie to ask her.

"Come on it'll be fun and the weather is going to be great," Jeffery begged.

"Everyone in the county will be there," Ramona added. "He's right; it'll be fun and Jessie isn't taking any time off from work, we'll have a good time," she said leaning over whispering to her friend.

"I don't know," Charlie whispered back to Ramona. "But, maybe it wouldn't hurt and maybe Jessie will start paying attention to me. It's not that big of a deal to go out with Jeffery just once and I'll be with you and Chandler," she said trying to convince herself. She turned back to Jeffery. "Sure," Charlie finally answered giving in.

"Great, I'll pick you up Saturday about five thirty. They're going to have some new games and of course, the hay ride. You'll see it'll be fun," he answered excitedly. He turned and walked away.

Saturday evening came quickly. She stood looking in the mirror. "Okay Charlie, you're going to have a good time and not let Jeffery get to you." She laid her hairbrush down on the dresser and continued to stare. She shuddered when she heard the car drive up and stop in front of the house.

"Good evening, Mrs. Bellamead. Is Charlie ready?" Jeffery asked standing so confidently peering in through the screen door.

"Yes, come in Jeffery, she'll be right down," Martha responded. She stepped back from the door allowing enough room for Jeffery to step inside the foyer.

"Good evening, Mr. Bellamead," commented Jeffery walking into the living room.

Everett nodded his head. "Good evening, Jeffery," he answered back. Everett's eyes squinted as he studied Jeffery.

Jeffery stood shoulders back so precise in his pressed jeans and expensive plaid shirt.

Martha stood at the bottom of the stair beaming with a huge grin on her face.

"Hi Jeffery," Charlie called out bouncing down the stairs letting her red hair fly, wearing her best blue jeans and reddish brown cotton sweater that matched her hair.

"Are you ready to go," he asked his eyes scanning her from head to feet. Charlie was one of the prettiest girls in the county Jeffery thought.

"Yes, let's go. We don't want to keep Ramona and Chandler waiting." She stopped by the front door. "See you later Daddy, bye Mom," she called out stepping out onto the verandah.
The crisp fall air made her shiver.

"Isn't it a beautiful night? Look there's even a full moon coming up," said Jeffery. He reached over putting his arm around Charlie leading her over to the car. He opened the passenger side door helping her into his pride and joy, a baby blue 1957 thunderbird convertible with its top down. She pulled her hair back with a ribbon and leaned back in the seat looking up into the soaring South Carolina pines standing tall pointing up to the sky. She could see darkness was overtaking everything with the sun setting giving off all the oranges and red in the sky overhead.

This wasn't so bad and maybe tonight would be fun. She

looked over at Jeffery. She smiled and thought that he was very handsome. Maybe her mom was correct and Jeffery was an okay guy. The car's radio played as a backdrop to Jeffery's stories.

The car turned off Main headed towards Jones's gas station. "I didn't get a chance to fill her up earlier. It won't take but a few minutes," Jeffery assured.

"Fill her up, Mr. Jones," Jeffery called out. "Do you want a coke-cola?" asked Jeffery walking over to the coke machine.

"No," Charlie answered. Something caught her eye as she looked over to the side. There standing in his torn blue jeans and worn dirty shirt in the station's bay staring at her with hurt in his face was Jessie. He looked down at the ground wiping a tool with a rag. He spun around going back to the car that he was working on. Oh, why did I come? She should've known that Jeffery would pull a stunt like this.

With a huge grin across his face, Jeffery hopped back into the car. "Alright, let's go. Look, the moon is getting brighter; it's going to be a great night."

She knew Jeffery had made his point to Jessie that Charlie was his at least for tonight and he'd won, since Jessie didn't say anything to stop him.

Charlie sat fuming, not just mad at Jeffery, but at Jessie. She never wanted to hurt Jessie, but why didn't he come over to the car and why had he been avoiding her? Why didn't he stop her and tell her not to go out with Jeffery? Jessie wasn't going to interfere with her dream of leaving or maybe it was his dream of leaving. Nonetheless, the pain was there in his face of how he felt about her being with Jeffery.

The parking lot was packed as Jeffery found a perfect spot to leave his car. Ramona and Chandler walked arm and arm up to them. Jeffery's arm slid around Charlie pulling her close to him leading them to the fairgrounds.

She felt horrible and wanted to run back to the gas station to let Jessie know that her feelings were still the same for him and she was so sorry she had hurt him, but it was too late. She was with Jeffery for the night and talking to Jessie wouldn't reverse the look in his eyes.

Words weren't going to help Jessie feel any better and she was sure he was more incentivized to move on with his life without her, now more than ever.

Lights flashed and music played pulling everyone into a world of fantasy. The Farris wheel sat in the same place as it did each year with its lights flickering. Jeffery helped Charlie into the seat as it swung back and forth. The Farris wheel slowly began to rise in the air. His arm wrapped around her shoulder bringing her close. He was now showing her off to the town, like a prize he'd won. At the top of the Farris wheel, she could see all the way to Jones's gas station.

A stabbing pain struck her heart. "Oh, Jessie," she whispered, "why didn't you come to the carnival? Why didn't you fight for me as you did at the picnic? This should've been our night." The answer was clear; Jessie wasn't giving up his dream of leaving this town, and she wasn't a part of that dream. She was glad the music was so loud and Jeffery was self-absorbed.

Later that night, Chandler and Ramona walked up to one of the booths to play a game. Charlie walked past them to next booth, the shooting game. "Alright, I want to give this a try," she said looking up at Jeffery.

"If you say so," Jeffery nodded in a confused look, handing the man his money.

Charlie picked up a few guns checking each one out as the man in the booth sneered at her, thinking he had a pigeon. A smile came on her face when she looked at the scope it was bent.

She chuckled. This would be like playing jacks with the old planks leaning on the porch, knowing she could win. Joshua had taught her all about guns and to check the scope to be sure it was straight. She placed the rifle up by her face and peered into the scope leaning her shoulder correcting the aim. She fired hitting every duck. The man stood stunned. She laid the rifle down.

"I'll take that brown small bear with the white feet," she said victoriously. The man grunted as he handed her the prize stuffed animal.

They moved over by Chandler as he finished his game with his strong arm throwing the ball knocking down all of the bottles. They started laughing when the bottles that were glued down to the table even fell off.

"Daddy, please win me a teddy bear," a little girl begged. Charlie turned around and watched the young couple not much older than she was. The mother shook her head no, but the daddy couldn't refuse his daughter. The daddy paid the man and picked up one of the riffles firing missing each shot. His face grimaced as he lay the rifle down.

"I'm sorry honey," he said. His body slumped looking at his wife.

"That's okay Daddy," the little girl said putting her tiny hand in his.

Charlie pulled away from Jeffery and circled around behind the daddy. She placed the teddy bear she'd won in his free hand not saying a word. He lifted up the bear, and squatted down by his daughter. Her face beamed as she grabbed and hugged the prized stuffed animal. The mom started to speak, but he shook his head no. His head turned and he smiled back at Charlie.

Charlie hurried back to Chandler and Ramona. Ramona smiled her sweet smile, but before she could say anything about what Charlie had done, Chandler handed Ramona a huge white stuffed dog.

The four slowly walked to the fairground's barn and through the large doors. Jeffery was on a mission headed to the animals in the back of the barn that smell of hay, animals, and leather. He stopped in front of all the animals with Montgomery Plantation written across the door. He stood as a roaster showing them all the blue ribbons the Montgomery Plantation had won. Of course, Jeffery and his father wouldn't accept anything less.

Ramona took off with Chandler in tow and Jeffery and Charlie followed. They walked past all of the crafts. Ramona stopped and peered up at the quilts hanging on the wall. Her eyes glistened in the lights looking at the wedding ring quilt, the blue prizewinner, a light cream quilt with pastel colored rings. Chandler's head bowed yes as he squeezed her tightly letting her know someday she could have any of the quilts she wanted.

Charlie walked down the next isle seeing the big blue ribbon sitting on the fried apple pies with Pearl's name across them.

Miss Ethel and Miss Mary Jane walked up. Jeffery grabbed her tugging her close. Miss Ethel smiled at them. "I declare, isn't this a nice fair! I see Pearl won again and I have to say she deserves the blue ribbon," Miss Ethel announced adjusting her thick glasses on her small round nose with her small beady eyes on them.

"Yes, it is a nice fair, Miss Ethel," Jeffery offered. He turned to leave. "Have a pleasant evening, ladies."

Charlie's heart sank. She understood before morning the women of the county would have her and Jeffery married off. Gossip would fly faster than a wild fire and this would stir up her mom. How could, one small date get so mixed up?

It was a perfect night with the full moon shining down, but not for Charlie. Her thoughts were of Jessie, not Jeffery. She tried to move away from Jeffery, but his grip was tight and he wasn't letting her go. She sighed wishing it was Jessie holding her, but that wasn't going to happen, not tonight and maybe not any night.

It was eight o'clock and the hayride was beginning. "Are you ready," Jeffery asked looking over at Charlie while Chandler helped Ramona into the worn hay wagon from the Johnson's farm.

"Sure." She nodded her head. Jeffery gently helped her up onto the hay. She settled in next to Ramona in the old wagon. The smell of hay and warm apple cider filling the cool, crisp air was soothing. Jeffery scooted in close to her, snuggling pulling her next to him in.

The aged wagon creaked rolling down the dirt road. The horse's hoofs clip-clopped in the quiet night headed to the Johnson's farm. Jeffery encircled Charlie's waist leaning his head down next to hers. She smelled his cologne. Her eyes looked up at Jeffery. His face nestled by hers, and he softly kissed her on the cheek. She knew if she stayed here in this small town her life would be marrying Jeffery and living at Bella Oak, not a bad life by no means. He was very attractive and living with Jeffery, she wouldn't have to work. They would be the wealthiest couple in the county. She would be a true Southern belle, but that didn't appeal to her very much.

It was odd sitting so close to Jeffery; her body didn't have any emotion stirring, so differently from when she was near Jessie. She closed her eyes remembering how her body tingled, feeling so warm next to Jessie. Her life with Jeffery would be passionless, empty, and cold. Could, she actuality live a life like that? She would never be able to love Jeffery as she did Jessie.

The night finally came to an end. She waved goodbye to Ramona and Chandler.

"Oh, this was an amazing night," Jeffery admitted grinning from ear to ear. He opened the car for her, closed it quickly, and then slid into the driver's seat. He turned the key, but didn't shift the car in reverse. He stopped and looked at her. "I have to admit. Chandler and Ramona sure looked happy."

"Yes, they are," she said softly looking at him. The car slowly drove through town. Charlie leaned back in the seat and began to hum along with the song playing on the radio. Then she couldn't catch her breath. *Will You Still Love Me Tomorrow* began to play.

The chorus kept playing in her mind seeing Jessie singing the lyrics to her. Her throat tightened and she fought back tears.

The car slowed turning through the huge iron gates of Bella Oak. Jeffery smirked looking up at the massive plantation home sitting high up on a hill overlooking all of its land. He grinned believing his dream that he had for years of marrying Charlie and moving in might be coming true. The car pulled to a stop in the circular drive and the music died. Jeffery helped her out of the car and he stood on the steps. He gently drew her close kissing her goodnight. She ducked her head and gently pushed away.

"Good night, Jeffery," she quickly added hurrying in the front door.

"Good night, Charlie. I will see you tomorrow at church," he affectionately called back. He strutted back to his car believing he'd won. The car circled around the old magnolia tree and glided down the long path and out the gates. Jeffrey's taillights disappeared into the night.

Charlie walked into the living room. Her father sat in his old chair. "Well, how was the festival and carnival," he asked peering over his book.

"It was very nice and of course, I saw Pearl's fried pies with their blue ribbon. The carnival was packed full of people since the weather was so pleasant. Everyone from the county was there."

"Everyone," he asked looking up at her.

"Maybe…not everyone."

"Well, it's getting late and we have church early in the morning," he said compassionately. He stood gently laying his glasses and book that he'd been reading on the end table.

"Daddy," She sucked in a deep breath. "Jessie saw me with Jeffery tonight and I could see how I hurt him, but he didn't say anything. Why didn't he stop me or say something?"

"Oh, honey," Everett said sympathetically. His hands grasped her shoulders looking into her face. "That's not Jessie's way. He ain't ever going to stand in your way 'cause he only wants you to be happy. You are going to have to be the one to make your own decision of what you want in life and tell him."

"But Daddy, I just wish I knew what my decision was and what I really want to do with my life," she added turning her eyes from him.

His eyebrows lifted.

"Goodnight, Daddy," she said.

"Goodnight, Charlie, it'll work out," he answered as they walked together up the stairs.

She lay in her bed trying to make some sense out of the night. So many options for her life; stay here, marry Jeffery, a passionless marriage, and live her life like her ancestors on Bella Oak, or move on to Atlanta…but neither option included Jessie.

Charlie knew deep down she didn't want to leave Jessie. How could she blend the two dreams of leaving town and loving Jessie? Did he feel like she did? Did he want to be with her or was his dream of leaving this small town more important? Why wouldn't he tell her he wanted to be with her? She lay in her bed looking out the window into the dark sky as confused thoughts of the evening played in her head.

CHAPTER 11

Thanksgiving

Jessie didn't talk to her the next few weeks and she believed he was giving her his answer. Leaving the small town was his dream, not being with her, and she would have to move on, live her life without him.

Thanksgiving Day was next Thursday and Martha and Pearl had invited the Ledford's to join them for Thanksgiving dinner.

That Thanksgiving Day was a cool, a beautiful morning. The Ledford's old black truck drove up in front of the plantation home. Jessie helped all the blonde, blue-eyed children leap from the back of the truck. Debbie was walking and Pearl quickly swished her up into her large arms, hugging her.

Jessie stepped up on the verandah. He stopped. His eyes peered down at Charlie and smiled. She bit her lip remembering the look of pain flowing through her mind from that night at the gas station. Jessie didn't speak. Pearl gave him a hug and everyone made their way inside the huge home. Charlie wondered if he would ever forgive her for going out with Jeffery. A wave of anger grew. Why didn't he say something that night or tell her how he felt? Why did he turn and walk away?

The table was set with the Bellamead's china and her mother's best tablecloth. The three families circled the table. Everett sat at one end and Jack at the other. Jessie sat down next to Charlie and when the prayer was said his hand reached over and took her hand in his. She touched his rough callused hand. Her body quivered. She gulped keeping the tears from flowing. These were hands of an artist not hands of a mechanic. She had missed him so much the last few weeks and knew that even though her secret dream of being with him might not ever come true, she still loved him.

Jessie couldn't hide his feeling anymore and softly caressed her hand. She felt pain stabbing her in her heart. Gently her fingers stroked his dry worn hands, knowing he did forgive her.

When the Thanksgiving meal was over Ramona and Charlie went down to the spring and Jessie went to his tree to sit quietly and draw. He stopped on the bank, looked down at her and smiled. She held her breath. For a brief moment, she hoped that he would lean over and kiss her again and would tell her how much he loved her. She wanted him to tell her not to ever go out with Jeffery again, but he turned not saying anything and went to the old tree up on the hill, their tree. Tears swelled in her eyes watching him walk away and thinking maybe he didn't want her in his life.

Ramona looked at her friend and shook her head no. "Charlie, Jessie is a different sort and holds his feeling in, a little like you, but he does love you, that I know for sure."

Charlie nodded her head yes agreeing with her, words wouldn't come. She thought about leaving Ramona for a while and going up to the tree to talk to him but she didn't move. She wanted Jessie to come to her.

CHAPTER 12

Decorating for Christmas

December came and that was all it took for Martha to begin planning her Christmas party that would take place Wednesday the twenty-first of December. Everett began bringing down boxes and boxes full of Christmas decorations from the attic.

The first Sunday afternoon the fourth of December, Ramona and Charlie began excitedly going through each of the Christmas boxes, just as they had each December.

"Oh, look this is the box full of angels," Ramona squealed softly holding one of the angels in the air. "This is my favorite box."

"Well, this is my favorite box," Charlie added, pulling out the different sized Santas and straitening their red coats.

"Oh good," Martha said briskly walking into the living room. "You can go ahead and decorate the mantles. That job we can get done now." She crossed the room wrapping her arms around Ramona. "Thank you again for helping to decorate Bella Oak for the Christmas party."

"Oh, I love to help each Christmas Mrs. Bellamead and you know how much I love angels. I should be thanking you for allowing me to decorate the mantel with them. I love my angel you gave me last Christmas; I already have her out in my room."

"Good, I also have a special present for you this Christmas, but you will have to wait for a few weeks," Martha added excitedly, hugging Ramona.

Ramona softly clutched a group of the angels in her arms going to the fireplace mantle in the dining room. An hour later each of the rooms, living room, and dining room began to turn into winter wonderlands, as the girls placed the Santas and angels in the perfect spots just as they did each year.

"Alright, next weekend, we will bring in the greenery from outside. The mantles will be perfect," Charlie declared waving her arms in the air.

Charlie stopped by the front window. "Look…Daddy and Joshua are putting the lights up on the house. Let's go watch," Charlie raced out the front door with Ramona following close behind her. She picked up a string of colorful bulbs the size of her hand softly rubbing the swirls. "Oh, I love these Christmas bulbs," she cried with delight. "They look like soft ice cream cones in different colors." She held onto the string of lights and hurried over to the ladder. "Daddy, do you need any help?"

"Sure, you and Ramona straighten out the strings of lights and give them to Joshua. That will help a lot," he added. "We sure miss Jessie. He's like a monkey climbing this ladder, and I'm getting too old to do all of this work."

"No, problem," Ramona assured, handing Joshua a string of lights. "We will help you, Mr. Bellamead."

"Now girls, next week after church, we are going out and finding us the best Christmas tree," Everett said climbing down from the roof. "How does that sound?" "Great," came the response from the two girls, their eyes peered up at the house full of lights. It would be wonderful to see them grow brighter in the darkening night.

Ramona lifted the last strand of lights up to Joshua. She stopped and spun around. "Oh, I better get home; it's getting late. Bye Charlie, Mr. Bellamead, Joshua."

"Bye, see you in the morning on the bus," yelled Charlie.

"Thanks for your help Ramona," called out Everett. His arm wrapped around Charlie walking back to the house. "She, shor' is a nice young girl,"

Ramona sat down next to Charlie on the school bus Monday morning. She sat quiet twisting her hands in her lap.

"Okay what's going on?" questioned Charlie.

"Oh, I'm so excited about the Dawson's Christmas party the twenty-third. I can't wait for you to see it. I have been helping Chandler's mom decorate the huge plantation home. Vanessa didn't want to do any work so Chandler and I picked out the tree and decorated it. I can't believe this is real."

"Oh, it's real and I can't wait to see the plantation decorated. I know everything will be perfect."

"Well, the party is going to be wonderful," Ramona said sighing.

"Then what's wrong Ramona?"

"I just wish I could get Chandler a Christmas present, but I don't have enough money, he told me not to worry about it, but I hate…" not finishing her sentence of being so poor.

Charlie eyes squinted and she sighed leaning back in the seat.

Sunday finally arrived and Ramona came running up from the spring. "Sorry, I took so long Mr. Bellamead, but I had to help Momma clean the kitchen after Sunday dinner."

"No problem, Ramona. Okay, let's go," Everett called out setting his saw in the back of the old black Ford. He opened the door and the two girls climbed into the truck.

The truck bounced along the dirt road out through the pastures. It pulled to a stop by the thick woods, the same place since the girls were little that they'd always found the perfect tree. "Now, this time try and pick a smaller tree. Last year it barely fit," he announced laughing. He stood by the truck watching the girls run through the woods searching to find the perfect, handpicked tree.

"Here, this is it," Ramona called out.

"Yes, that's the one! Oh look Daddy, c'mon hurry," Charlie yelled.

"Charlie, it's not going anywhere, calm down." He stopped next to Charlie and studied the tree. "Well," he laughed, "that shor' is a fat tree full of limbs." He put his hand to his mouth, pondering as the girls wiggled with anticipation.

"Well, Daddy?"

"Yes, it's a little fatter than last year's tree, but your mom is going to love it." He leaned down and began to saw. "At least you two have grown and I don't have to drag the tree alone," he assured.

The truck bounced to a stop and Martha stepped out on the verandah, a big grin on her face. "I see they got their way again." Her head shook back and forth. "I thought you were going to bring back a smaller tree this year."

Joshua came from the barn. "Here, let me help you, Everett," he called out climbing up into the truck. He leaned his head back and began to laugh looking at the large fat tree.

"Don't say a word, Joshua," Everett whispered sideways.

The two men cleaned the tree and placed it in its spot right in front of the large living room plate-glass window, the same place where the Christmas tree had rested for generations, giving off the smell of Christmas cedar throughout the house.

"There, how do the lights look," Everett asked, stepping down off the ladder. "Next year you two are doing the lights or we are getting Jessie to come over here and string them." He sat down in his chair resting while Joshua took the ladder and put it away.

"It's perfect, Daddy. You do such a good job. You know where to place the Christmas lightbulbs to make the tree sparkle," Charlie offered. She reached in the box full of ornaments. "I love these colorful ornament balls. They're so bright and shiny when the light from the bulbs hits them.

"Well, I love the cutout ornament balls with the different miniature scenes of Christmas in them. They each tell their own story," Ramona said. She giggled. "I love the ones with the tiny snowmen inside."

"Oh, look this box has all of the ornaments we made over the years," Charlie declared. She carefully lifted up some of the homemade ornaments.

Ramona sighed. "You don't have to put the ornaments I made on the tree. Mine aren't as good as yours and Jessie's," Ramona said looking down at one of her uneven homemade ornaments in her hand.

"Yours are just fine, Ramona," Martha assured. "It wouldn't be our Christmas tree without all three of your ornaments and you both have to make more ornaments this year when school is out." She sat down in the rocker by the fireplace slowly pushing it back and forth.

"Okay, we just have to hang the tinsel." Charlie beamed slapping her hands together. She handed Ramona some tinsel and laughed as they threw it up in the air letting it sail down onto the tree sparkling with the lights reflecting on it giving off the look of colorful ice cycles.

"Lordy mercy," Pearl proclaimed coming out of the kitchen carrying two mugs of hot chocolate with marshmallows. "That is the prettiest tree I have seen in a long time."

"Thanks, Pearl," they both replied taking the mugs.

They sat on the worn oak floor in front of the Christmas tree sipping on the warm chocolate. Their eyes fixed on the lights glowing red, green, orange, blue and a few creamy white, the most beautiful tree they had in years. The aroma of the tree was so pungent bringing back memories of when they were small waiting for Santa.

"Ramona, why don't you play a few Christmas songs? That's my favorite part of Christmas," Everett assured, pulling out and lighting his old worn pipe.

"Sure…Mr. Bellamead," Ramona answered. "Here Charlie, you can help decide which songs." She sat down at the grand piano and the beautiful music flowed, as her small hands softly touched the keys. *Silent Night* and *What Child is This*, Everett's favorite tunes as the girls began to sing.

"Alright," Joshua hollered coming into the foyer. "Yes sirree, now it's Christmas!" he insisted sitting down in a chair. Pearl came into the room handing him some hot chocolate. She sat down on the sofa and began singing along with the girls.

The fire flickered in the fireplace the tree blinked almost keeping time with the music. The old grandfather clock in the foyer bonged. Ramona stopped playing. "Oh, I better get home; we have school in the morning. Just a few more days, and then…Christmas vacation."

"Ramona, before you go…here," Everett announced, standing up out of his chair. He pulled out some money from his pocket. He lifted her soft hand placing the money in her palm. "You have helped around this place for years and never taken any money."

She started to say no, but he stopped her. "Now, girl, don't start that foolish pride of your poppa's. You take this and buy whatever you want for Christmas."

She closed her mouth and smiled. She reached up and gave him a hug and her eyes swung to Charlie. She now could buy Chandler something special for Christmas.

"Thank you, Mr. Bellamead. I appreciated it," she said clutching the money tight in her hand.

Charlie walked down to the spring, half way to Ramona's home, since it was dark. "Oh, Charlie this is going to be the best

Christmas ever," Ramona declared, spinning around giggling, holding onto her money. "I am going to buy Chandler a special gift. Oh, our first Christmas together and I hope the first of many," she wished.

"Yes, it is and I can't wait for Christmas either," Charlie called back watching her friend go across the rocks on their dam.

"Bye," Ramona yelled, stopping on the other side of the creek waving. "I will see you in the morning on the bus," as she ran up the hill to her home.

The next few days zoomed by. Wednesday morning the school bus stopped in front of the large gates of Bella Oak and Charlie climbed on, but instead of Ramona getting on the bus and sitting by her, Jessie sat down. "Ramona has a cold and isn't feeling well. That old house is too damp and cold. Mom is calling Dr. Miller and he is coming out later. She wants you to get her schoolwork and bring it over."

"Sure, that won't be a problem. Jessie, we don't have a lot right now. She seemed fine yesterday at school."

Frown lines grew on his forehead. "I don't know what happened, but she was up coughing most of the night." He shook his head. He leaned back in his seat exhausted with work and school not getting enough rest.

Jeffery climbed the steps of the bus. He stopped when he saw Jessie sitting next to Charlie. Jessie smiled and put his arm around Charlie.

For the next couple of days, Charlie brought Ramona's schoolwork home, but Ramona wasn't improving. She had bronchitis. Dr. Miller believed with rest over the weekend she would be better by Monday.

CHAPTER 13

Ramona

Monday morning the nineteenth of December, Charlie was collecting her schoolbooks. A loud knock at the front door startled her. She swung the door open and Jessie stood in front of her his eyes were swollen and face drawn.

"Jessie, what's wrong?" She asked terrified.

Everett stood from of his old chair and walked up behind Charlie.

"Red, Mom, and Dad took Ramona to the hospital last night, she has pneumonia, and I couldn't go since I had to stay with the little ones. I wanted you to know before you went to school. She is real sick with a high fever."

Pearl walked up. "Who is with the children?"

"Brother John's wife is staying with them until I get home and the twins aren't going to school, today."

"Well, I'll go stay with the children," Pearl said, grabbing her things.

"Then, I'm going to the hospital, if that's okay, Pearl?" questioned Jessie.

"Yes, you go ahead we will be fine. I'll take care of the young'uns," Pearl replied.

"How are you getting to the hospital, Jessie," Everett asked.

"I don't know sir, but I will find a way. It's not too far to walk. I walk home many nights from the gas station."

"You walk from town?" Everett's voice rose.

"Yes Sir."

Everett shook his head. "Here." He handed Jessie keys. "Take the old truck over there, no one uses it and it has a full tank of gas."

"Daddy, can I miss school this morning and go see Ramona at the hospital?"

"Yes," he answered making his own decision, as Martha silently stood behind him.

Charlie grabbed her books and lunch and hurried out the door with Jessie. She'd go to school that afternoon. She climbed into the old 1955 black truck. Jessie put the truck in reverse spun the truck around and they bounced down the dirt road in silence. He pulled up and parked in front of the small, creamy-white-brick, county hospital. Jessie held the door and they went into the lobby and over to the elevator.

The elevator dinged and they stepped out and began to walk down the hall. Jessie stopped walking. His parents walked out of a room. Jack was holding onto Grace who was bent over sobbing with tears streaming down her tired face. Charlie's heart pounded and she couldn't catch her breath. Jessie ran and she followed. Jack shook his head no to his son.

Grace looked up her hand reached out to Charlie. "Oh Charlie, she loved you so much," she cried out, her body quivered.

"What, do you mean…she loved…me," Charlie asked terrified.

"I am," Jack's voice cracked, "sorry to say she passed away a little while ago," Jessie stood trembling. He spun around grabbing hold of Charlie.

"She died very peaceful in her sleep," his head swung. "She just couldn't fight," Jack answered, hesitatingly. He turned and led Grace to a chair.

Jessie pushed open the door. He held onto Charlie and walked into the cold stark room. Ramona laid on the bed her blonde hair surrounding her pale face. She looked so…peaceful.

Jessie walked to one side and Charlie walked to the other side of the bed staring down at her. He reached out and gently took his sister's hand leaning down, caressing it.

Charlie stood her entire body shaking looking at the pain in Jessie's face, watching tears drop onto Ramona. She felt like someone had punched her in the stomach and she couldn't seem to breathe. It was as if someone's hands were gripped around her throat choking her. She gulped for air. This couldn't be real, her best friend lying so quiet. She leaned over.

"Oh…Ramona, please wake up," Charlie whispered. "I can't live without you. Who will I tell my deep secrets? I can't make it without you. Please…wake up." She wiped the tears from her eyes. Gently she touched Ramona's hand not wanting to let go. Maybe if she held onto Ramona's hand she would come back to her. This couldn't be real and maybe this was a horrible dream. She felt as if she was dying along with Ramona. Her own life was being sucked out of her as she looked down at her sweet friend. Every emotion was overcoming her body: love, anger, fear, sadness, and anxiety. The thought terrified her to live without Ramona. The two of them had been inseparable their entire lives and no one knew her so well. What was she going to do? She stood still holding onto her best friend's hand. How would she ever let go?

Jessie wiped his tears and slowly walked around the bed. He wrapped her in his arms. "Red, you have to let her go. I have to let her go. Her light has left us," he whispered softly. He sucked in a deep breath, the hardest words he had ever spoken, as he squeezed Charlie tight. She felt his body heaving, trying to be strong for her.

"We will be alright, and she will always be part of us," he whispered holding onto to Charlie for support.

Charlie placed Ramona's soft sweet hand back onto the bed. She turned to Jessie understanding how hard this was on him. He and Ramona were so close and had confided in each other their whole lives. She wanted to be strong for him, but she couldn't quit sobbing. This was a nightmare. Jessie led her out of the room. Dr. Miller was standing over by his parents and they walked up to them.

"Dad," I'm going to take Red home and stay with her for a while."

Jack just nodded his head yes, not able to talk.

This time they walked down the spiral stairs to the lobby and out the front door. The office ladies in the office bay quit their work and looked toward them with solemn, sympatric expressions. Jessie helped Charlie into the old truck. She didn't even remember the drive home.

The truck pulled up in front of the large plantation home. She felt numb. She climbed from the truck and looked up at the beautiful Christmas lights around the large plantation home. This was Ramona and her favorite time of the year. This was supposed to be their best Christmas ever.

Martha heard the truck pull up in front of the home. She stepped out onto the verandah and Everett came from the barn, instinctually knowing something was wrong. Charlie ran to her mom throwing herself at her, sobbing.

"No!" Martha bleated, looking over at Jessie. "No, it can't be," she cried out, hugging her daughter with tears running down her face. "Not Ramona, she had too much life."

Pearl hurried to Jessie grasping him. "I'm so sorry," she sobbed holding onto him. "Don't worry, Miss Hannah is with the children."

Everett and Joshua walked up. Tears were in their worn eyes. Everett grabbed Jessie. "I'm sorry, son; let me know if I can help in anyway." He stood and looked Jessie in the eye. "Son, it is alright to cry. Your tears are from God and it is fine to let them flow. It is a way for you to cleanse your soul. Don't be ashamed of your tears," the old man assured with tears running down his tired face.

Jessie stood in front of the man with tears flowing. "Take care of Red, she needs you now," he begged. "I have some things to see too. May I borrow the truck again?"

"Son, you can have that old truck. Maybe Jones can help you keep it running. We'll see to Charlie. I mean it I'm willing to do anything to help," Everest said patting Jessie on his back.

Jessie walked over to Charlie. "Red, I have to leave for a while, but I will be back later," he added softly. He didn't move until he was sure she was all right. He gently wiped her tears from her face.

She grabbed him. "Jessie, don't leave. I can't lose you too."

He hugged her with all his strength."I will be back, I promised." He smiled at Charlie.

Charlie watched the old black truck back out and turn to leave with its taillights blaring red. Her mother led her into the house. Charlie stopped walking and looked over at the Christmas tree. She gently touched the tree. Her eyes stared down at the ornaments that Jessie, Ramona and she had made. "We didn't get to make our ornaments this year," she sniffled holding onto a limb of the special tree Ramona had picked out. "What am I going to do without her? This can't be true."

Everett went to the cabinet in the dining room and pulled out a bottle of bourbon, pouring a small glass. "Here Charlie, take a sip it will help calm you down."

She shuddered as the warm liquid ran down her throat. It burned.

"Now lay back on the sofa." Evert spoke in a quiet voice. Martha sat down by her daughter and put a throw over her. The bourbon made her drowsy and she lay there hoping this was a horrible dream. Finally, she drifted off to sleep. Charlie woke and saw her dad sitting in his chair, his face blank staring at the Christmas tree. She knew this wasn't a dream.

"How do you feel?" he asked.

"I don't know," she offered. "Daddy, this has to be a bad dream. Ramona can't be gone. She has always been with me; she wasn't supposed to leave like this. She wanted to stay here in this county and marry Chandler. Oh, Chandler, do you think Jessie will tell him?"

"I'm sure he will."

"She was going to marry Chandler and live on his plantation and have a bunch of blonde-headed kids," she sniffed trying to catch her breath. "She had so many plans. Oh, Daddy, why would God take her away from us, when she was so young?"

"Charlie that is a question men have been asking since the beginning of time and there ain't no good answer. At lease we know she is in Heaven. She was a Christian and there wasn't anyone kinder than her." His body inhaled trying to stay composed. "Now your mom has made you some vegetable soup and fresh biscuits. You need to eat something," he said leaning down helping her up.

Charlie grabbed her daddy and sobbed.

"Oh, Charlie…this is one thing that I can't fix for you. I'm here for you, but we are all going to have to ride this out in our own way," he sighed leading her into the kitchen.

"Oh, honey, you are awake," Martha wiped her tears and gave her a hug. "Here try and eat a little it will make you feel better. You know Ramona would be the first to tell you to take care of yourself."

Charlie ate a few bites, but the food wouldn't go down her throat. "Where's Pearl?"

"She went over to the Ledford's to help out with the children and took them some food. I'm making a casserole and some cookies, and I'm baking some fresh rolls later today for them.

Charlie knew her mom's way of handling everything was baking, no matter what the problem.

"Thanks Mom, for the soup." She stood scooting her chair back under the table. She felt numb. "I think I will take a walk and get some fresh air."

"That's fine, if you need me I will be right here," Martha added sympathetically. She busily moved back to the stove, pulling her apron up wiping the wetness from her face.

The screen door squeaked as Charlie softly closed it behind her. Before she stepped over Betsy, she leaned down and petted the dog's head seeing those brown eyes looking up saying how sorry she was with her tail softly hitting the ground. Charlie slowly walked and without thinking she made her way to the spring. She stood and listened to the soft flow of water over the dam. She didn't know if she could come back here without Ramona, but something had tugged her.

She crossed the creek and walked up the hill sitting on the other side of the bank was Jessie his sketchpad in his lap drawing.

He looked up, "Red, I came back by your house earlier but you were sleeping."

"Daddy gave me some bourbon and I guess it put me out. Do you mind me sitting down? I didn't know if I could come back here."

"Come on over here and sit down. Ramona wouldn't like you staying away from this place. I know this was her favorite place in the world and she will always be part of it," he said wiping his eyes with the back of his hand.

"Oh…Jessie this is so hard and I don't think I can carry it."

"Red, you and I will be able to go on. I can feel her with us and see her big smile," he said patting the grass by him for her to sit down.

"This was our special place since we were little and you're right she will always be here in spirit. Jessie…I won't look at your drawing, you don't have to stop." She sat down next to him wiping the tears looking at the crisp sparkling water flowing in their extraordinary place.

"That's alright, you can look. I was drawing this for you and I'm about done." He did a few more swishing with his pencil. Gently he tore the page out of the tablet and handed it to her.

There, on the soft white paper was a picture of Ramona and her sitting on the bank by the spring with the water slowly flowing over the dam of rocks.

"Oh Jessie," she whispered tenderly a feeling of calmness overcoming her body, "it's as if Ramona is sitting right here. The drawing is so realistic I can feel her and can hear the water flowing from the drawing, just as it is doing now. This is amazing, thank you," she said softy as tears dropped onto the paper. Jessie leaned over hugging her. She looked up into those blue eyes. He leaned down and kissed her on her forehead as she cuddled next to him, finally feeling safe and not so lonely, knowing Ramona would be happy.

They sat talking about all of the good times of their past that they'd had sitting and playing down by the spring over the years. They made a pack they would never forget them whatever happened in their lives. They knew their lives would always be twisted together no matter what. It was beginning to get late and reluctantly Jessie stood. His hand reached down pulling her close, softly moving her wild red hair from her face, kissing her. She didn't move looking up into those blue eyes she adored and wouldn't deny her feelings.

CHAPTER 14

Saying Goodbye

Charlie shivered in the cold afternoon. It was December the twenty-first. This was supposed to be the day of Bella Oak's Christmas party, not the day to say good-bye to Ramona. The wind softly blew as the winter sun peeked serenely through the trees, a perfect backdrop for Ramona.

Peering over at the Ledford's and so many others who had gathered, Charlie stood next to her father. The tiny cemetery was full of people wanting to say goodbye to a lovely girl. Everett had insisted that Ramona be buried in the family cemetery at Bella Oak, since he considered her family. She loved the plantation so much, and he wouldn't take no for an answer, not this time.

Charlie stared across the cemetery at the graves of her family, remembering not long ago when they stood here saying goodbye to her grandmother Charlene. But that time, Ramona was standing next to her. Years ago, Everett and her grandmother Charlene had planted bushes of jasmine and gardenia around the cemetery. There was an old oak tree over to the side that shaded the graves from the afternoon sun.

Jessie's eyes met her eyes. Her heart was being torn apart and the lump in her throat was choking her. She wanted to run to

Jessie, to hold onto to him, and not let go, but she stood still hoping that she would be able to do that someday. The preacher spoke his words, but they didn't seem to make it to her ears and the group began singing *Amazing Grace*, one of Ramona's favorite songs. The preacher prayed and the service was over. With tears blurring her eyes, Charlie stood, but was not able to move. She wanted to scream, "No this isn't over! We can't leave." But, she knew she must.

Ramona's family stepped back allowing everyone to walk by to tell them how sorry they were for their loss, and to say their last goodbyes to Ramona. She saw Chandler walk up. He bent over the grave covering his face with his huge hands sobbing. Jessie stepped up grabbing him. It was difficult watching Chandler touch the casket saying goodbye to the young girl he loved and had planned a life with.

Pearl and Joshua walked up. Pearl leaned over kissing little Debbie on the head and then hugging Jessie. Now, it was Everett and Martha's turn to walk up by the Ledfords. They stood there both wiping their eyes. Everett grabbed Jack and the two men hugged. They weren't worried about what anyone thought. This was hard on the two men both feeling as if they should have done something to save Ramona.

A silence fell over the cemetery. Now it was Charlie's time to say good-bye and everyone stepped back, but Jessie. She leaned down and touched the beautiful casket. "Ramona, I will visit you often and I know you will always be at the spring with me. I will always love you." Her voice trailed off as Jessie held onto her. His hand touched the casket. "Sis, I will take care of Red, but we promise never to forget the times we had together. We love you. I love you."

Charlie looked up at him. "Jessie, I can't leave her here like this," she sobbed. "Please don't make me go. Someone has to stay with her. We can't leave her alone."

Jessie grabbed her tighter. "Yes, you can. She is in Heaven, and you are here with me. We will be alright; she wouldn't want you to be in so much pain."

He looked over at the casket and softly whispered again, "We love you, sis." He stepped back leading Charlie to the side of the cemetery to allow his parents a chance to say goodbye.

Pearl walked up.

Jessie looked down at Charlie, he whispered. "We will make it, Red. Ramona wouldn't want you to be so miserable. I will meet you down at the spring as soon as I can get away, but don't tell your mother," as he ushered her to her parents.

Charlie stood paralyzed staring at the grave. She knew she had to walk away leaving her best friend. Her eyes landed on Chandler. She drew in a deep breath knowing he felt as she did, not wanting to go. Her daddy grabbed her; she tugged to a stop and turned looking back at Ramona's grave. She whispered, "I promise I will come back." It was the hardest thing she'd ever done leaving Ramona there that cold day. She looked over and Jessie was watching her giving her the wink he used to give Ramona, the sign that she would be okay.

Everyone meet at the plantation later in the day to have supper. Martha knew the Ledford's home wasn't big enough for all of the people from the county that had showed up to pay their respects for Ramona. It was difficult for everyone knowing that this was not the Christmas party that the town's people had wanted, but Martha wanted a celebration of Ramona's short life and this was Ramona's favorite time of the year.

Martha walked to the record player in the living room and put some Christmas music on. Some of the women gave her a strange look, but Christmas music was appropriate because that was what Ramona would want, Christmas music flowing through the old plantation home. Chandler sat in a chair in the living room listening to the music and watching the lights on the tree. A small smile grew on his face remembering Ramona laughing putting up Christmas decorations. He understood what Martha was doing.

The next few days were hard. Charlie seemed to go through the motions of Christmas, but without joy. She would always remember the good times, just as Jessie and she had promised their beloved Ramona.

CHAPTER 15

Christmas Angel

Christmas day was approaching. Charlie gave Jessie his present of drawing pencils along with a sock hat and gloves, remembering the winter before he had worked outside in the cold with his hands freezing.

One morning right before Christmas, Martha stood crying in front of the Christmas tree holding a gift in her hand.

"Mom, what is wrong?"

Her mother turned around. "This is Ramona's present I bought her in Charleston last spring. Ramona loved angels as much as I do." She slowly opened the gift pulling out a beautiful angel that looked like it had come from Heaven dressed in its pure white gown made out of silk.

"Oh, Mom," Charlie cried out, "that is beautiful! Ramona would have loved that angel."

"Well, now," she sniffed carefully placing the angel in the dining room on the mantel, "she is an angel and more beautiful than this one." She wiped her tears.

Charlie left her mom in the dining room and went for a walk down to the spring. Jessie was sitting there on the bank absorbed in his thoughts as she walked up. His head was down in his hands and he didn't see her walk up.

"Jessie, are you alright?" she called out worriedly.

"Oh, Red," he said looking up. "Yes, I'm just tired of being poor. I'm sorry, I couldn't buy you a Christmas present. I'm sure you got a nice gift from Jeffery." His tired blue eyes looked at her.

"Jeffery gave me a box of chocolate candy and some flowers, and Pearl and Mom enjoyed them both. She scooted in by Jessie taking his callus hand in hers. "Jessie your present was the best ever."

"What present? I didn't give you one," he asked confused.

"Yes, you did and I will always cherish the drawing of Ramona and me," she assured pulling him close. "Don't you understand money can't buy everything," she whispered. She gently pushed his hair from his eyes feeling the scar on his forehead.

"I guess I have a lot to learn," he tenderly said, leaning over giving her a kiss.

"Jessie....why didn't you say something that night at the gas station when I was with Jeffery," she asked looking down playing with blades of grass.

"Red," he answered pursing his lips. "Your mom stopped by the gas station one evening to get some gas. She let me know in a few words that you were going out with Jeffery and for me not to interfere."

"What!" Charlie yelled standing up.

He reached up pulling her back down by him. "Now don't say anything to her. She means well. She loves you very much and wants the best for you, and she doesn't believe I'm good enough for you." He stopped. "I see in your face that she's had this conversation with you before, too. Right? She wouldn't want us meeting down here. If you talk to her about this, she will watch you every minute."

"Yes," she shook her head. "Mom is all for me marrying Jeffery, but I think I should set her straight."

"On what? You are still leaving and so am I, but at least we have some time to spend together." He reached over pulling her close. "Now, are you going to be quiet?"

"Yes," she added snuggling next to him, "but someday…"

Jessie interrupted, "*Somedays* are a waste of time. We have to live our lives now."

She knew what he meant; Ramona didn't have any *somedays*.

CHAPTER 16

Their Last Goodbye

January first came and they welcomed in the new year of 1961. This year there wasn't any celebration as in years of the past. Ramona had always spent the night, and the two girls would stay up until midnight, so excited about ringing in each New Year.

Charlie sat on the bank watching the water trickle over her rock dam. "Happy New Year, Ramona," she said softly looking into the still water.

"Happy New Year, Red," Jessie said. He briskly bent down kissing her, making the New Year official. Official, that was all Charlie felt. She had made no plans and no resolutions. The cold, gray, dripping days of January flowed into February with only more overcast and chilly days.

One cold winter day in February, Charlie sat staring at her reflection in the creek water. She smiled seeing Jessie's reflection in the still water standing over her. "Don't laugh," he begged apprehensively as he handed her a tablet of drawings. "You promised you wouldn't laugh, remember?" he reminded her as he sat beside her.

She took the tablet in her hands and carefully flipped through the white soft pages seeing beautiful pictures of her and Ramona playing in the spring. There was one of her sitting in the old twisted live oak tree after the Fourth of July picnic, the day she had realized she had fallen in love with Jessie.

A tear of joy slipped down her face. "You are so talented and should never hide your work. These are amazing." She gently hugged the tablet tight. "Please, promise me you will never stop drawing. I mean it! No matter what happens." Her eyes stared into his blue eyes.

He gulped. "I promise to keep drawing, but I will only show you my work. You can have those drawings if you would like."

She leaned over touching his face and kissing him. "Thank you, this is the best present anyone has ever given me and I will keep them forever."

Their time together was precious since Jessie was always working. He had the afternoon off one cool day in February and led her over to the old oak tree. He reached over with his hand helping her climb up to their favorite limb. She smiled touching his new warm gloves looking up at his blue sock hat, but grimaced looking at his worn winter coat as she snuggled close to him.

"You know," she said cuddling, "you will have to take some time off from school to come to Atlanta to visit me after you start college. Mr. Kent said you were getting your scholarship for next fall, so your plan is working."

Jessie sighed. "We'll see how things go, but I will visit you in Atlanta." He said picking up his tablet drawing.

She cinched up her mouth in dissatisfaction. Why was he always changing the subject and not talking about going to college?

She sat back against the old tree watching him draw. He flipped the page and began to draw the old plantation home with Charlie and Ramona sitting in the swing on a warm summer day. It was amazing how she could feel Ramona sitting next to her telling her dreams of marrying Chandler as she watched the picture come to life. Jessie carefully tore the drawing out and handed it to her. She gently took the drawing in her hands holding onto it like a treasure.

Months went past, May came, and with it graduation. Jessie, Jeffery, Chandler, and Billy Mac were graduating from high school. Jeffery had already signed up for college. Chandler was staying on his ancestral plantation. Ramona dying had taken the life out of him. He wasn't the same bubbling, sweet boy anymore because his dream of life with Ramona would never become a reality.

The end of May, Everett sat back in his chair after supper. "I talked to Jack today and found out why Jessie isn't going to college this fall. He worked all year at that gas station and paid off the hospital and doctor bills. He even paid for Ramona's burial on his own and didn't want his father working in town. He wanted his father home with the family. He is an amazing young man," he added looking over at Charlie. "I offered to help, but neither one would accept any money. Jessie has that foolish pride just like his father."

Now, she understood why Jessie had been upset about not being able to buy her a present for Christmas and why he wasn't talking about leaving for college. She assumed he would stay another year and he would keep working at the gas station until he saved up enough money for college. A part of her was happy he would be right with her for a while. She wouldn't be alone and she wouldn't have to make any decisions about her future, not yet.

It was the first week of June and the coolness of the spring air mixed with the warmth of the sun. Charlie leaned back on the bank of the creek remembering last summer. Her memories of Ramona flowed like the water. Ramona pulling off her shorts so she could go swimming and Jessie getting onto her about swimming in her panties. She could see Ramona clearly in her mind as she floated with her long blonde hair swaying in the spring water.

"Hey," came, a voice from behind her, "I thought I might find you here. I've got some news, but I wanted to be the one to tell you," Jessie said. His face became solemn.

"Oh, Jessie you're going to college," she squealed looking up at him.

"No, not quite," he said sitting down by her nervously twisting his hands together. "I joined the US Army yesterday."

"The Army!" She leaped from the ground and stomped her feet.

"If I stay in the Army long enough, I can attend college, it's the only way for me to go."

"No, it's too dangerous! Daddy said he would give you the money for school."

"I can't take any money from your father," he said looking over at her playing with a stick and drawing pictures in the dirt.

"Oh, you and your stupid pride."

Jessie moaned.

"You are going to get yourself killed and then I'll be all," she paused and quietly spoke, "alone."

"But, you're moving to Atlanta when you finish high school next year." He shrugged his shoulders. "So why does it matter to you if I stay or not?"

"It – just does," she snapped tears built in her eyes.

He leaned over and pulled her close. "It won't be that long and you can write me and I will send you my drawings of where I am. We both said we weren't staying here and you will be leaving to go to Atlanta before you know it."

"I'm going to miss you so much – so very much."

"You just come down here and sit and think about me, and you won't be so lonely. I will keep drawing you and the spring, and then I'll be able to make it."

"When do you leave?"

"This Saturday," he took in a deep breath.

"Two days," she sniffed wiping the tears building in her eyes with the back of her hand.

"Yes, but I'm not working so I will be able to sit here with you – until it's time to go."

Tears finally gushed down her face. Jessie's fingers gently wiped them. She stared into his blue eyes that she'd fallen in love with.

"One, thing," his mouth stiffened for a second, "I want you to stay away from Jeffery. Don't mess your plans up of leaving the county. Don't let your mom convince you to marry him. One of us has to succeed with our dreams. Do you promise me?" he asked staring into her eyes.

"Yes, I promise, I will be glad to stay away from Jeffery. My dreams will come true and so will yours. You will become a great architect someday," she whispered holding onto him. There was that word again, *someday*. "I have confidence in you, Jessie Ledford!" Charlie proclaimed, dismissing the notion that someday would never come. Both shook their heads in agreement and continued to embrace.

Early the next morning, Charlie walked down the path to the spring where she found Jessie waiting. She stopped and quietly studied Jessie. His face was taut, as he looked into the gently flowing water. What was her life going to be like without him? She wanted to tell him her new dream of wanting to marry him and never letting him leave, but she was too stubborn and it was too late. He looked up and smiled his special smile telling her that she would be all right.

He reached out with his hand. She put her hand into his and he pulled her close.

"Red, I can't hold back anymore. I love you. I have always loved you, and it's so difficult to leave."

She leaned over putting her hand on his face. "Jessie, I love you too. You are and will always be my true love," she whispered putting her lips on his not worrying about her mom or anything. She leaned back on the cool grass next to Jessie their bodies tangled. Her body trembled nervously for a few minutes throbbing with sensations she had dreamed about. She knew this time she wouldn't be able to stop herself. She touched his wild hair with her hand swishing it from his face feeling the scar over his eye wanting to remember everything about him.

He pulled her tight, knowing this was their fate. His hand slid down her body. Waves of sensations took over. An avalanche of emotions took over their entwined bodies. Her nervousness disappeared and their bodies became one, their passion, their love taking over for each of them.

They laid there on the bank of the old spring creek the rest of the afternoon telling each other their deepest thoughts and dreams. They knew their lives were threaded together no matter where life took them. They both were young, but had learned a difficult lesson from Ramona. *Life* isn't endless.

Saturday arrived.

Charlie stood on the verandah with her dad, mom, Joshua and Pearl. Jessie shook hands with Everett and Joshua; but the men both grabbed and hugged him. Martha said goodbye with her true feelings showing, tears in her eyes, but proud. She believed that this was for the best; Jessie needed to leave and move on with his life.

Pearl stood quiet, not able to stop tears dripping down her plump face. "Jessie you take care and remember how much we care about you," she said handing him a small package. He grinned as Pearl continued, "Yes, that is my fired pies, and you better come back soon to get more." She gave him a kiss on the cheek.

Jessie turned to Charlie. "Let's walk down to the spring," he said wrapping his arm around her not paying any attention to her mom.

They stood by the dam they'd built. He gently wiped her tears and softly kissed her. "I know our lives are going different directions, but Red, I will love you tomorrow and always."

She looked up into his sparkling blue eyes that were filled with tears.

He gulped. "Your dad said I should never be ashamed of tears because that is how God cleanses the soul. I will come back to you and I do want to stand here by this spring with you with joy in my heart," he added gently wiping her tears.

"Jessie, I love you and I will love you always. Please come back soon," she whispered kissing him one last time.

Jessie took long steps up the hill that summer day, wiping his eyes, leaving Charlie standing by their beloved spring. She watched him disappeared over the hill and she could hear the old truck leaving down the dirt road and out the gates of Bella Oak. She stood frozen in place but felt shattered to the core, like a statue ready to crumble to the ground. She was alone with only the memories of the mighty oak, the rippling spring, and the rock dam to hold her together.

CHAPTER 17

Someone Watching

The morning of July fourth, Bella Oak was dressed in her glory for the Fourth of July picnic. Her balloons and banners of red, white, and blue colors flowed across the verandah. Cars parked on the grass that lined the drive and family after family talked and walked slowly around the yard bringing laugher back to the old plantation.

The same small group of young people sat quietly on the verandah, but this year everyone wasn't joking around, teasing each other, or laughing. Chandler sat to the side of the porch with his head bowed remembering last year's Fourth of July when he finally was able to talk to Ramona. Jeffery sat arrogantly in the swing and his eyes panning the old plantation with a confident look on his face. He believed that he had won Charlie since Jessie was gone.

At lunchtime, Charlie sat next to Jeffery eating her barbeque at the long table under the huge oak tree with her friends. Her eyes stayed on her father. He had a big smile across his face as he told his old stories to Jack Ledford who was sitting next him. Neither of the men paid any attention to Mr. Montgomery. Grace was busy telling all the women how proud she was of her son, how well he was doing in the Army, and that she believe he would be coming home soon.

After they were full of barbeque, the small group of friends by habit made their way down to the spring. Billy Mac leaped into the spring splashing Carol. She squealed happily with her eyes only on Billy Mac. Jeffery stood still giving his sister a disapproving look that she continued to ignore.

LeAnn swam near Chandler splashing him trying to get his attention. Charlie had to finally smile watching the old fun-loving Chandler coming back smiling and talking to LeAnn.

The day of dealing with Jeffery was getting to Charlie. She climbed from the spring and hurried up the hill to the old oak. Hearing a noise, she stopped walking, and turned around. There standing about a foot from her was Jeffery.

"Oh, that is some oak tree," he said taking one more step next to her. "Charlie, you've been crying."

"I just miss Ramona," she said wiping the tears from her eyes. "Jeffery, what do you want?"

"I just wondered where you were going," he leaned over pulling her close. "I hate seeing you so sad. I can help make things better if you would give me a chance, but you keep running away from me."

"Jeffery, I just need some time alone."

"You know, Charlie," he began with his arms wrapped around her. "I do love you and I'm not going to give up on us. Our lives could be perfect. You just need to give us a chance," he said gently, lifting her face up to his.

She tried to pull away but Jeffery held onto her tight. This was his chance to prove to her how much he loved her and he wasn't going to give up easy.

"Wow, what was that?" he asked.

"What?"

"Something hit me on my back."

"Oh, maybe an acorn hit you."

"No, it was a hard hit, like someone strong punched me in the back," he turned around peering down the hill. "Over there, see that shadow running up the creek bank. Someone was watching us.

"No, I don't see anyone."

"I'm telling you that there was someone here, I know it."

"Well then we need to get back to the spring," she said turning to leave. She stopped walking and turned back to the creek. Her eyes stared into the grove of trees on the other side. She gasped when she saw the same shape of a shadow she had seen that day with Hudson, someone was out there watching and protecting her.

"Thank you," she whispered wondering who it was.

The Fourth of July picnic finally ended and the plantation became quite. Charlie pushed the swing on the verandah back and forth and stared at the old oak tree sitting up on the top of the hill next to the creek.

"Who is watching me," she whispered to herself. She took in a deep breath. "Thank you, whoever you are."

CHAPTER 18

Happy Birthday

Days, weeks moved on, and each day become more difficult for Charlie missing Jessie. Why didn't she stop him from leaving? If she had only told him how she felt months ago, he might not have joined the Army? She knew she had so many why's in her short life. Why didn't she tell him that October before she went out with Jeffery that she wanted to go out with him? Why didn't he tell her about her mom stopping by the gas station to inform him that she had a date with Jeffery? They had wasted time that they could have spent together. She had made up her mind as soon as he was home she was telling him she didn't want to ever live without him and would live wherever he wanted.

August the twenty-ninth arrived, but this year the weather stayed calm and Charlie's birthday was quiet, too quiet, no hurricane in sight.

"Happy Birthday, Charlene," Martha said. "When you finish your breakfast do you mind this morning running to Piggly Wiggly? Pearl needs a few items to finish up for your party."

Charlie slid the kitchen chair out and sat down. "Sure, where's Pearl?" She asked as she spread butter and fresh honey on her biscuit taking a big bite letting the honey ooze out.

"She's picking some peas for supper tomorrow night. Ya know that she's always busy," Martha said, squeezing fresh ground hamburger into plump round patties for the party.

"You and Pearl have done too much for this party. I didn't even need one."

"Yes you do. Now, here's the grocery list. You can take your daddy's truck. I have my car full of clothes for the yard sale at church next week."

Charlie placed her plate in the sink and washed it along with the glass. She dried her hands on the hand towel and picked up the list and truck keys. "I'll be back in a little while."

She stepped out the front door. "Happy Birthday, Charlie," her daddy said leaning forward in the rocker. "It's hard for me to believe you're seventeen. Most of your friends will be here for your party," he said looking sadly up at the verandah's light blue ceiling.

"They'll both be with me, too," she added, smiling back at her father. "I have Jessie's drawing he sent me for my birthday, the drawing of my birthday party with everyone here including Ramona."

He nodded his head agreeing.

"Daddy, why is life so hard. I should have listened to you about Jessie and told him sooner how I felt? Did you know that Mom told him not to interfere with Jeffery and me? That was why he didn't say anything to me that night of the county fair."

"No, honey, I didn't know, but your mom loves ya so much. She was only trying to do what was best for you. We can get mixed up and let events detour us off the path we should be on to get where we want to be."

She nodded her head.

"Honey, ya only need to follow your heart and use a little common sense and you'll be fine. Happy birthday, Charlie."

"Thank you, Daddy. Well, I need to run into town for Mom. I'm taking your truck."

"Here," he added reaching into his pocket, handing her some money, "she needs gas. Eli will fill her up for ya."

"Bye, Daddy," she called out jumping down the steps. "See you in a little while."

The truck started and she slowly drove down the dirt road and turned onto Second Street. The truck jerked to a stop next to the pump at Jones's Gas Station.

"Charlie, what a nice surprise! I thought it was your daddy," old man Jones said, hobbling out to the pumps.

"Mom needed me to run to the grocery and Dad said to fill her up for him."

"That, we can see too," he leaned over near the window. "You know Jessie is a good worker, but his heart wasn't in it to become a mechanic. But, that boy, he shor' did work hard. Have you heard from him?"

"Yes sir and he is doing fine."

"I shor' have been worried about him, but maybe this joining the Army won't be so bad after all."

"I hope not, but I'll be glad when he's back home," Charlie agreed.

"Yep, me too…Billy Mac," he yelled over to the station bay. "You come and fill Charlie's truck for her." He turned back to the window. "Now that boy right there is a good mechanic, and I hope he stays awhile," he chuckled, turning going in the station's door.

"Happy birthday, Charlie," Billy Mac said connecting the gas nozzle to the truck.

"Thanks, Billy Mac. Are you coming to the party?"

"I sure am. Eli said I could take some time off," he wiggled his head nervously. "Is Carol going to be there? I haven't had a chance to talk to her. Jeffery has been keeping a close eye on her," he added ducking his head down.

"She's supposed to be at the party." Charlie leaned her head out the driver's window. "Is there something going on with you and Carol?"

He finished putting the gas hose back on the pump. He turned around and moved close to her. "You ain't going to tell anyone, not a soul….."

"No," she whispered.

"Well, Carol and I have been sneaking around seeing each other for the past few months. She sneaks out at night and I pick her up at the gate of the Montgomery Plantation."

"Wow, you're taking a big chance. Mr. Montgomery would be furious with you if he finds out."

"I know, but you won't tell anyone. You promise, right? I jus' needed to tell someone."

"Of course not, and I think it's great. I wish Jessie hadn't worried about what my mom said. We wasted so much time that we could've spent together. Now, what can I do to help?" she added squinting her eyes thinking.

He squeezed his hands back and forth. "Maybe jus' talk to Carol. She shor' is worried about her daddy."

"I'll do better than that. Jeffery is always around, but maybe at the party I can keep him busy for you. Soon, he will be going off to college and will be out of the picture with football, and all."

"You would do that for us?"

"Sure."

"But…Charlie, I know you can't stand to be around him. I've watched you."

"Yep, but I'll see what I can do. Stop worrying. I better get going. Pearl needs some things from the grocery."

"You shor' don't want to keep her waiting." He stepped back from the truck wiping his hand on a rag. "I can't wait to eat some of your birthday cake. Peal does know how to bring out the best food in the county."

"Bye, Billy Mac," Charlie said starting the truck. "Bye, Mr. Jones," she called out waving her arm out the window at the old man standing in the doorway.

She finished her grocery shopping and headed home. Her mind flowed full of memories. The old truck bounced along the dirt road and turned into Bella Oak. The sun was shining through the old oaks and her daddy was still sitting on the verandah waiting for her.

She told her daddy what she had planned to help Billy Mac and Carol and that this would make her birthday special.

"Well, hanging out with Jeffery will make your mom happy," he said laughing.

"I'll write Jessie and tell him what I'm doing. I don't want someone else writing to him telling him that I spent lots of time with Jeffery at my party. That'll make it okay."

That afternoon she did as she promised and kept Jeffery busy making him feel special, letting Carol and Billy Mac sneak off and spend some time together. She smiled knowing all hell was going to break loose when Mr. Montgomery found out about Billy Mac and Carol. She did hope the two were prepared. Another kind of hurricane was brewing at this year's birthday.

CHAPTER 19

News

The first of November arrived and Charlie and Everett sat in the swing on the verandah swinging back and forth as they made plans for the holidays. Everett's feet stopped the swing. Jack drove up in his old truck and parked in the circular drive. The door squeaked as it opened and he climbed out of his truck, his head down, and reluctantly he stepped up onto the verandah.

Everett stood up.

Jack's face was drawn. He stared at Charlie.

"Jack, what's wrong? Is one of the children sick?" asked Everett.

"No Everett," he nervously said handing him a note he held in his trembling hand, his eyes on Charlie.

"No, this can't be true!" Everett yelled, his eyes fixed on the man standing in front of him.

Jack bowed his head yes and tears flowed down his worn face. When Everett yelled Martha and Pearl came rushing out of the house.

Joshua raced from the barn. "What's going on. Everett?" he called out hurrying up onto the verandah looking at the faces of the two men.

Everett turned back to Charlie, "Honey," he began and Pearl began to cry. "This here note is from the Army. It says that Jessie is missing in action in Vietnam," he gulped, "and presumed dead."

The words hit her like someone stabbing her in the heart taking the life right out of her. She struggled to breathe. No, this couldn't be happening. She sat back down in the swing paralyzed with pain. Her eyes peered up into her father's green eyes. Her body didn't feel anything as time stood still.

"We are so sorry, and this time let us help if you need anything," Joshua pleaded. He looked up at Pearl. Her body was trembling and tears were running down her face. Joshua reached over to her. He held onto Pearl as they went into the house.

Martha hugged Charlie and held on to her, but before they went inside the house, Jack stepped near her. "Jessie loved you, girl, since he was a young boy. I saw his pictures he drew back when you were a little thing. Drawing pictures of you is what started that boy drawing and what has kept him drawing his whole life."

Charlie reached over hugging the man with blue eyes just like Jessie's. "I know, and I have always loved him and will always love him. But, Mr. Ledford, I don't believe he is gone. Someday, I know he will be coming home. They don't know," she added letting go of him.

There was that haunting word again, *someday*. The next few weeks, Charlie wasn't giving in. She believed Jessie would be coming home. End of discussion.

The families gathered for Thanksgiving, but this year the dinner was filled with sadness.

The room was cold and the food choked her, each bite of food was difficult to swallow as she thought about the two empty places at the table. She looked at her daddy and he bowed his head telling her she could leave.

She stepped over Betsey that was lying by the back door, and Charlie walked down her path with her arms hanging down by her side gripping her fingers tightly closed. She entered into her magical world of the creek. She stopped, listened to the birds chirping overhead, and the water flowing down the stream. She crossed the dam and kept going up to the hill where the majestic old oak tree stood. She reached up grabbing one of the old limbs with her hand pulling herself up on one large limb at a time until she reached as high as she could go.

"Oh, Jessie, where are you?" she called out with voice echoing over the land. "Please come home to me."

She sat against the high branch remembering his touch as he held onto her hand helping her climb up next to him. "I know that you are out there and coming home to me. Know that I'm waiting and I'll always love you.

CHAPTER 20

Billy Mac & Carol

It was Sunday morning, November the twenty-sixth and Charlie woke to voices that she heard from downstairs. She sat up in bed trying to listen. She finally gave in and ran to the stairs. There standing in the foyer was Carol sobbing dressed in her pajamas with Martha holding her. She looked up as Charlie raced down the stairs.

"What's going on?" Charlie called out.

"Charlie," Carol turned towards her, "Daddy found out about Billy Mac and me, and I don't know what he is going to do. He took off after him."

"What?"

Everett came hurrying down the stairs. "Don't worry Charlie," he said patting her on the back. "I'll go and find Billy Mac and Zach. I'll try and calm things down."

Charlie hollered, "Let's go to my room, Carol." She closed the bedroom door and jumped on the bed. "Okay, what happened?" Charlie asked pulling her legs up under her.

"Oh, it was Jeffery! I knew we shouldn't have tried to go out last night with him still home from school. I made it back to my room early, I didn't even stay out that late, thinking all was well." she sniffled.

Charlie threw Carol a box of tissues.

"Early this morning I heard Jeffery and Daddy talking and then Daddy started yelling. He said he was going to kill Billy Mac. Charlie I think he means it. I begged him not to hurt Billy Mac." She sighed, "I even promised not to see him again, but he wouldn't listen."

"Don't worry," Charlie offered. "Daddy will find them, and it'll be alright."

"I knew this was going to happen, but I was hoping not for a while."

"Did you call Billy Mac and warn him?"

"Yep, but he was going to stand up to Daddy." Carol leaped from the bed and began to pace the room. "Oh, I can't believe my own brother told on me."

"You knew how Jeffery felt. Sorry Carol, but he is a snobbish fool."

She laughed. "Yep and he still thinks of you like some kind of trophy he can win. Not that I would mind your being my sister-in-law, that would be great! But, I know how much you love Jessie."

"Here's a pair of jeans. Get dressed. Just pick one of my sweaters to wear."

"The waiting is driving me crazy," Carol shuddered. She slipped on the jeans pulling a sweater over her head. Her fingers combed through her hair. "Boy I'm a true mess."

"Go to the bathroom and wash your face, and you'll be fine."

"Okay," Carol replied. She used a little of Charlie's makeup to cover her puffy eyes and put on some lipstick.

Carol bounded out of the bathroom. "Let's go downstairs. We need to see if your mom has heard from your dad."

The girls walked into the living room and Martha was sitting in the rocker, sipping her coffee.

"Mom," called out Charlie, "have you heard anything from Dad?"

"No, but I'm shor' worried; that Zach is a stubborn man."

"If you hear from Daddy let us know. We're going to the kitchen to get something to eat."

Martha clutched her coffee cup tight nodding her head yes.

Charlie pulled out some cinnamon rolls that Pearl had made the day before and put a couple in the toaster oven. She retrieved a bottle of Borden milk from the frig sitting it on the kitchen table.

Her hand reached for a glass in the drain board. She gasped and the glass slid from her fingers crashing into the sink.

"Charlie," her mom yelled from the living room, "are you alright?"

"Yes. Mom, I just dropped a glass. I will clean it up, no problem."

Carol flew out of the kitchen chair. "Charlie, what's wrong?"

Charlie didn't answer. She just opened the back door and Billy Mac stepped inside.

Carol ran throwing her arms around his neck. "Oh," she moaned letting her hands fall down. "Daddy's still looking for you? How did you know I was here?"

"I figured you'd run to Charlie," he laughed. "She's the only friend that would face your daddy down."

"Now, what are you going to do?" asked Charlie.

"Well," Billy Mac grinned his face blushed. He bent down on one knee. "Carol Ann Montgomery, would you marry me?"

Carol didn't move for a second, then she whispered, "Yes."

"You know," he assured looking down at the ground, "what you are doing giving up on the life you are accustomed to. I don't make a lot of money at the gas station, but Eli said he would let me buy it from him," Billy Mac sighed. "He's getting too old to run it."

"We'll make it. Mrs. Baker said she loves how I sew and has always wanted me to work for her in her dress shop, but Daddy wouldn't let me. Come on let's go before Daddy or Jeffery finds us. Jeffery will know I will run to Charlie, too."

"I hid the car down at the old service road, but it's cold out do you have a coat?"

"Oh, my coat is in the foyer."

"I'll get it," Charlie said, cutting through the kitchen door to the foyer. She rushed back and handed the coat to Carol.

Carol grabbed her. "I," she sniffed, "always wanted you to be at my wedding."

"Well, I will be in spirit, but you better get going or there won't be a wedding."

"Thanks, Charlie," Billy Mac quietly called back to her leading Carol out the kitchen door. He stopped and turned around. "You know you are going to get in trouble."

"Yep. Ain't it great," Charlie whispered, smiling.

She watched out the kitchen window over the sink as Carol and Billy Mac ran through the woods to Billy Mac's car. She hoped they would get away.

She took in a deep breath and sat down. She looked toward the living room where her mom was still sitting in her old rocking chair sipping her coffee. Charlie realized she would have to face her with the truth at some point. "Oh Lord," she smiled. But, that could wait a while. She cleaned up the broken glass and tossed it in the trash. Then, she poured herself a tall glass of milk and leaned back in the chair eating her cinnamon roll.

CHAPTER 21

Christmas Party

The first of December did arrive and Charlie, Billy Mac, and Carol did survive, but not without some bold admonishments. But, what was done was done. Billy Mac and Carol moved into the small apartment in the back of the filing station and Eli was proud to have them around, since he had never had any children and his wife had died years ago.

Charlie's life continued with her father bringing down the Christmas boxes from the attic, preparing Bella Oak once more for its annual Christmas party. She bent down opening the box of angels and carefully placed each one just the same as Ramona always did.

She lifted the new white angel out of its box and sat it in the center. "Oh, Ramona, please find Jessie and bring him home to me," she whispered softly, with a tear dropping onto the angel.

The next couple of weeks she stayed busy helping her mom and Pearl. The Christmas party at Bella Oak was going to be on the twenty-second of December since Martha believed they all needed to stay busy keeping the traditions of Christmas alive. The fresh aroma of cakes and cookies filled the large home along with the evergreens.

That Friday the twenty-second, Jeffery drove up in his blue thunderbird. He jumped out of his car, hurriedly gave Martha a Christmas present of beautiful flowers, and carefully sat Charlie's blue wrapped Christmas present under the tree. He caught Charlie off guard when she was standing under the mistletoe and gently pulled her close kissing her. This kiss was more than a simple kiss. The rest of the day he stayed by Charlie's side as much as he could with Miss Ethel and her group of gossips whispering about planning a wedding for Charlie and Jeffery for June.

After a few long hours, Charlie finally escaped and went down to the spring to sit. She shivered in the cold and pulled her coat up tight. She heard a voice and looked up, believing it was Jeffery, but there standing up on the hill was Chandler.

"Charlie, I hope you don't mind, I saw you leave the house and thought this might be where you were heading. I also needed to get away," Chandler added his face moist from tears.

"Sit down, Chandler. You know this was Ramona's and my favorite place to sit. This is where we started meeting when we were very young." Charlie ducked her head. "She loved it down here and if the creek was to full of water, before we put the large rocks in for the dam, she would sit on one side and I would sit on the other and talk." Charlie became quiet. "This was Jessie's and my favorite place too. Oh, Chandler I miss them so much." She took in a deep breath watching him wipe his eyes with his large fingers.

He leaned back on his hands. "Ramona told me stories of the two of you sitting down here that is why I knew where you were going. Charlie it's hard this time of year. Ramona loved Christmas and had so much fun decorating the plantation with me.

Charlie clinched her fingernails tightly letting them bite into the palm of her hands trying to hold back tears.

You know," he stopped for a moment, "I was going to ask Ramona to marry me this Christmas. I was hoping to have the wedding next June when she graduated high school. Charlie how can plans change so much?" he asked. His eyes peered up and he squeezed his hand together so tight the knuckles turned white.

"Chandler, I don't know, but I do know she was going to say yes to you. She couldn't wait to get married and have a bunch of blonde-haired, blue-eye kids. At least both of your dreams were the same. I know you would have made her very happy."

"Yes…" he sighed looking down at the ground.

"Now," Charlie threw a stick into the creek, "we have to move on. Ramona and Jessie wouldn't like us sitting around being sad. Ramona loved Mamma's Christmas party and always was right there with my mom planning everything and of course, playing the piano. Christmas music made the house feel so warm.

Chandler smiled. "My dad bought a baby grand piano last Christmas. No one in our family plays the piano but when he heard Ramona play the piano at church one Sunday morning, he had to buy her one. He was going to surprise Ramona at our Christmas party. He had put a huge red bow on top, just for her." He wiped his eyes. "That was her Christmas gift from my parents….a piano."

"Oh, Chandler," she began, "she would have been so happy. That was one of her dreams to have her own piano."

"Well I know she has the best music now," he said looking up into the blue sky with his voice breaking up.

"She sure does and I can hear her singing too. I can feel her down here with me at this spring. I just have to close my eyes and listen."

"It is peaceful here. Charlie, we better get back to the house as you said Ramona would be upset at us missing the party. I will stay close to you and keep Jeffery away if you like?"

"That's a deal. Let's go." Charlie jumped up from the ground and stared up at big Chandler. She took hold of his arm and they slowly walked back to house not talking just thinking of their memories.

Christmas Day was difficult. Charlie opened all of her Christmas presents even the one from Jeffery a beautiful bracelet with a heart on it with both of their names. Her mom and Pearl began to cook Christmas dinner and she slipped up the stairs. She carefully lifted up the first picture Jessie had given her the one of Ramona and her sitting at the spring. She held the drawing carefully next to her heart knowing this would always be the best Christmas present ever.

•••

The next week Everett walked into the living room. "Well, Charlie," her Daddy said, "a new year, 1962. This is the year of your graduation from high school, the year you are planning on leaving Bella Oak and moving to Atlanta. This is going to be a good year for you young lady. Start planning to make your dreams come true. Jessie would be proud."

"Yes, I will make my dream come true, at least one of our three dreams will come true. But Daddy, when I leave, I will miss you so much."

"Well, we still have a few months and Atlanta isn't that far away. You know you can come home often. I don't think you could stay away from Bella Oak for long. I know how much you love this old plantation and your mother will come and visit you. Enough of that for now. Happy New Year, honey."

"Happy New Year, Daddy," she said. Her daddy's big old arms reached over pulling her to him making her feel like a little girl again. It was a safe and happy place to be.

CHAPTER 22

The Snowman

On Valentine's Day, Charlie woke up to lustrous brightness filling her room. She quickly leaped out of bed and stood at the window. In front of her was a white winter wonderland. She raced down the stairs. "Mom, it snowed!" she shouted.

"Yes, honey, it did. Everything outside is covered," her Mom called back, laughing. "There isn't any school today; you know they shut down the whole town if there is a snowflake in the air. Come and eat your breakfast. I made you some pancakes and bacon."

"Can I go out in the snow for a while?" Charlie asked. "How much snow did we get?" "Sure, you can go out, but put plenty of clothes on and wear your leather gloves and good boots to keep your feet dry." Martha turned back to the stove. "Your dad said we got about seven inches, a very nice snow. It is so beautiful in all of the trees and my holly bushes are amazing and have their red berries surrounded by the white flakes."

Charlie gobbled her breakfast. She dressed in layers of clothes. She laughed when she tried to bend over to put her boots on feeling like she did as a kid. She stepped out the kitchen door and rushed off down the path to the spring with her camera hanging to her side. She wasn't giving up that Jessie would be coming home and he needed to see how beautiful the creek was with snow on top of the rocks in the dam and the frozen water glistening through the cracks of the rocks.

She slowly made her way up the hill to her favorite oak tree and turned to look down to the immense plantation home draped in snow with smoke from the chimneys swirling up to the sky. She looked up at the large towering cypress trees standing to the side of the home covered in white. This was a true winter wonderland. She stopped and clicked another picture for Jessie.

She walked up the hill looking up at the one, lone, giant magnolia tree standing in the center of the circular drive in front of her home with its large branches covered in white looking like a giant Christmas tree. It was the perfect spot for a snowman. The world was quiet that morning. Its pure white blanket had put the trucks and cars and tractors all to sleep. Suddenly, she heard squeals coming from across the way at the Ledford's home. She smiled recognizing the twins and Debbie screaming and laughing playing in the snow.

She worked endlessly finishing up her special snowman in the center of the circular drive placing bright blue buttons for his eyes and a carrot for his nose. Her daddy stood the entire time staring out of his office window watching her. He held up his cup of hot coffee and nodded his head telling her the snowman was perfect.

"Hey girl, that's some snowman," Joshua hollered, coming around the house. "I figured you would be out here. Now, let me take a picture of you standing by Mr. Snowman, before he begins to melt."

"Thank you, Joshua."

"Oh, I almost forgot. Pearl sent me to tell you she is making snow ice cream and it will be ready in a little bit. You need to come over to the house. You know Pearl won't venture out in the snow; she is a true Southerner." He laughed. "I love the snow. It makes the world so fresh and clean and it'll also help the fields as it slowly melts into the ground. See you in a few minutes, Charlie."

"Tell Pearl I will be over after I change clothes and get warm," she called back to him as he disappeared around the side of the home. Her eyes stayed fixed on the old oak tree up on the hill across from the creek, sitting so proud with its massive limbs ridged with snow.

That evening after supper, she sat quite with her parents by the fireplace, watching TV. When they heard the old truck of Jack's drive up and come to a stop out front. Everett stood from his lounge chair and went over to turn off the TV. "Oh, I hope there isn't any more bad news," he mumbled going to the door. "Hey, Jack, come on inside out of this cold."

Charlie held her breath. Jack didn't usually come over unannounced unless something was wrong.

"No, stop worrying," Jack assured walking into the warm room. "I jus' have a story I needed to tell Charlie," he added with a smile. "Grace and I sat looking at the snow yesterday and thinking. She went and pulled this old tablet out from the closet. I know, ya'll will remember the last big snow storm we have about twelve years or so when the kids were little." He nodded his head at Charlie. "I think Charlie you and Ramona were in the first grade. Do you remember?"

"I sure do," Charlie said, "Jessie and Ramona came over and we built a big snowman. Jessie had to have it perfect, with the head just the right size and the perfect blue buttons for his eyes and an old hat he got from Pearl. We had so much fun that day."

"Oh yes, ya'll did. I had told the kids that they could go outside for a while, but it got quiet, so I went out looking for them. They weren't anywhere in the yard, so I walked down to the creek. There, lying across the creek, was a two by six old board that they had placed over the water. I was furious, knowing they could fall into that cold rushing water. I stayed there by the creek fuming getting madder and madder waiting for them to come home. I finally heard them talking so I moved up on the hill to watch as Jessie helped Ramona across. I stepped out of the shadows, and you should've seen the look on their faces when they saw me with my arms crossed. I was so mad that I chewed them out all the way home. Once there, I stayed outside, but I let them go into the house with their momma to get warm. Once I calmed down, I realized that I was really more relieved than mad."

Everett started laughing. "I remember that day and I was thinking the same thing. How did, the two of them cross the creek. I followed them back down to the creek and saw what they had done. I stood on our side of the creek and watched them cross to be sure they made it safe, too."

"Well," Jack began, again with a smile. "Grace took me to the side one night a few weeks later and brought this tablet with her. "Jack," she said, "do you want to see what drove Jessie to go to Bella Oak." I sat there as she flipped through the tablet. This one tablet is full of drawings of you, Charlie. There are a few of Ramona with you, but manly you playing out in the snow. That day Grace told me about all of the drawings Jessie did. They were of you and he wasn't going to miss watching you play in the snow that day, no matter what. Grace and I want you to have this here tablet. She isn't ready to give the others up, not yet anyways," he said handing the tablet to Charlie.

Charlie's trembling fingers flipped through the pages. It was like a slow movie of that snow day from the beginning of their playing and building the snowman. At the end, the last page there was the three of them standing by the perfect snowman.

"Thank you, Mr. Ledford, and you tell Mrs. Ledford that when she is ready, I will take the other drawings, but I understand her needing them." She clutched the tablet, giving him a hug.

He stood wiping his eyes. "Well, I better be going. Ya'll have a nice evening."

Everett stood. He grabbed his coat and walked outside with Jack to the truck. Charlie watched as the men talked for a while and both kept dabbing their eyes with their white handkerchiefs. She held the tablet tight and walked up the stairs.

"Oh, Jessie, you will always be with me." She smiled down at the drawings in the tablet of memories of a special day which had been tucked away somewhere inside her for a long time.

CHAPTER 23

Everett

It was Saturday, March seventeenth, 1962. Charlie was helping Pearl hang out clothes on the old clothesline in the backyard. Shouting came from the side field calling for help. Charlie raced through the fresh tilled dirt running as fast as she could toward the call for help.

"Charlie," yelled Joshua, "go back and bring the truck!"

She spun around, ran back to the house, and grabbed the truck's keys. She quickly jumped into her father's truck bouncing over freshly plowed rows.

She swung the truck's door open and rushed to her father lying on the ground. "What happened?" she yelled.

"I don't know; I found him lying here," Joshua yelled back. "Help me get him in the back of the truck!" She grabbed her father's feet and the two of them lifted Everett up into the back of the pickup. Her father was taking in shallow breaths. Joshua climbed into the back of the truck next to Everett holding his head. He yelled at Pearl who was running down one of the plowed ditches. Get Martha and meet us at the hospital. Let's go girl!" he yelled."

Charlie drove faster than she had ever driven in her life. She pulled up by the emergency room door at the hospital. Two men ran out of the building and lifted her father out of the back of the truck onto a gurney. Charlie and Joshua followed them inside the cold stark building and sat down by the door in the hospital waiting room.

"Charlie, Joshua what is going on," Martha called out hurrying into the room.

"We don't know Martha. I found Everett lying on the ground....I don't know," the old man uttered, ringing his hands together.

A nurse walked over to them. "Mrs. Bellamead, Dr. Miller will be out soon to talk to you," she replied.

Martha sat down by Charlie and nervously crossed her arms squeezing them tightly.

Dr. Miller stepped out of a room gripping Everett's chart in both hands. "Martha, Everett has had a stroke and we are moving him to a private room." The man sighed. "It's not good." He shook his head. "He can't talk, but he's awake. You can see him in a little while," he added patting Martha on the shoulder.

Charlie saw in the doctor's eyes, a friend of her father's since they were children; her father wasn't going to live much longer. She gulped trying to hold back tears. She was a Bellamead and would be strong for her father just as he would want.

The small group rode up the elevator as Charlie had done with Jessie that day to see Ramona. They walked into another cold room. The same stabbing pain she had before had returned. There, lying so still was her father in the white bed with tubes and lights shining down on him. His green eyes stared up at her.

Charlie walked up to her father and softly stroked his hand. "Daddy, I love you so much. Don't worry, I know that you love me." He tried to mumble, but words that made sense wouldn't come. She was going to be strong; nonetheless, her feelings were overtaking her body. She leaned over and kissed him on the cheek.

Tears gave way and flowed down her face. "Daddy, I know you are a fighter. You just think I got my stubbornness from Grandma Charlene, but it really came from you. I love you. Don't give up. Please keep fighting Daddy! I need you," she whispered. She turned to leave, but stopped. She looked back one last time at her father. His eyes followed her out the door. Her hand grabbed the doorframe and she ran back in to hug him one more time. When she let go, she stood up and walked slowly back to the door. She stopped and stared back at her father. They both knew it was the last time for them to say goodbye.

When she got to the hallway, she saw that Jack and Grace were there. Grace reached out to her and led her over to a chair. Martha went in Everett's room and sat holding his hand. Joshua and Pearl sat next to Charlie while they waited. None of them would leave as time moved on slowly. Just as the sun set, Dr. Miller and her mom stepped out of the hospital room. Charlie saw the look she had seen before. She knew her father was gone. Joshua grabbed her mom as Martha wept uncontrollably.

Joshua, Pearl, and Martha left in her mom's car. Charlie stood in the parking lot by her daddy's pickup. She leaned onto the door and wept. She wanted to get as much of this sickening feeling out before she started to drive home.

Jack walked up. "Are you are alright to drive home," he asked?

"Yes, I guess. Thank you Mr. Ledford," she answered."

He gave her a hug. "Charlie, we're going to make it through this with God's help."

She nodded and then opened the truck's door and slid inside. She sat there and collected her thoughts before starting the truck. This time she didn't race down the road but drove slowly entering the massive gates of Bella Oak. She really didn't want to go in the house without her father there. How would she be able to go on without him?

People were already gathering at the house that day. News travels fast in small towns. She pulled the truck up to the old barn and park. Reluctantly, she got out and walked up the steps to the verandah. Everyone began to grasp her. Jeffery reached over and wrapped his arms around her not letting her go. This was more than she could take. She pushed his arms away and dashed to the kitchen. She was out the back door like a flash and headed to the creek.

She sat on the bank lit up by the moon staring into the water. "Oh, Ramona, I wish you were here. I need you so much. My life has turned into a mess," she whispered into the cool air. Tears dripped into the water making small splashes. She leaned back on the moist grass. She smiled. She felt Ramona's presence.

Her dad and Ramona wouldn't want her to give up. She had to keep going. She knew the two of them believed in her and they both understood her love for Jessie. They also would always be with her so she would never really be alone.

Thoughts of her father, grandmothers and grandfathers of the past, growing up on this old plantation, sneaking down to the creek swimming just as she always had done flowed in her mind joining the sound of water flowing.

The old spring creek drew her in like refreshment in the summer and tranquility in the winter. She stared down into the water. This was her serine place, her and Ramona's sanctuary from the world. She finally gave in, stood, and wiped her clothes off making her way back to the house. She didn't want to talk to anyone, especially Jeffery. She slipped up the back stairs to her room and she pulled out Jessie's tablet. She flipped to one of the pages where he had drawn a picture of her daddy and Joshua sitting on the porch in the rockers. She softly tore the page out of the tablet and carefully hung it on her wall. She lay back on the bed holding onto the special tablet. She closed her eyes and felt so close to Jessie, and she knew that wherever he was that he was thinking of her this very second. Looking up at her father's picture made her so proud and thankful.

A few days later, she was standing in the old cemetery saying goodbye. Now there were three people there who she wished could have lived on and on: her grandmother Charlene, Ramona, and Everett her dad.

"Daddy, I love you and tell Ramona how much I miss her. I miss you so much, but I won't ever give up on life just as you said that day on the verandah. I will come out here and keep things cleaned up just as you always did. I guess it's my turn now to see to this plantation. I promise to help Mom. We will be alright." She whispered as she touched the casket, "I love you." She stepped back from the gravesite to make room for her mother. Joshua stepped up and gently led her to the side of the cemetery.

Charlie looked over near the old oak. Chandler was standing by Ramona's grave with his head bent down and tears flowing off his chubby cheeks. This time he didn't seem as sad knowing that time does heal all wounds even the losses of the heart. Chandler would never forget Ramona, but he would live his life just as Charlie chose to do.

Days moved on and she helped her mom see to everything, the funeral, the life insurance, and the business of the plantation and transferring of names on property, but she knew things had changed with the loss of her father. Her mom had the life taken out of her and Charlie understood how she felt. It was like losing a part of their hearts and souls. It was difficult to keep going, but Charlie had promised her father to help with the plantation and her mother, and she'd never go back on her promise.

May had arrived bringing in a hint of summer. The warm sun shone down on the ground flickering through the oaks. Charlie and her mom sat in the old swing looking out onto her mom's garden. She could see that the small new green plants were pushing their tiny leaves up through the warm dirt. Life was moving on and

Charlie's hidden dream of moving to Atlanta to live and work in an air-conditioned buildings seemed farther and farther away.

Life had become confusing for Charlie. She didn't know which way to turn she was being pulled in so many directions. Stay here, marry Jeffery, and live on Bella Oak or move on with her dream of seeing the world. Her mom was all for her marrying Jeffery and living right here, but she still had her dream of leaving. Her plans were twisted in a knot and she didn't know if she could untwist them.

Charlie needed to clear her mind and there was only one place that she knew of that would help her. She grabbed her saddle and walked out to the pasture and over to Midnight, her horse that her father had given her years ago. She leaped on the horse and galloped across the pasture and over hills that were covered in old oaks and tall pines, where she and Midnight stopped. She stood silent not moving for a few minutes. It was a perfect spring day with the breeze bearing hints of jasmine and gardenias. She tied Midnight to the old large oak tree to the side of the cemetery. Slowly, she made her way to the two graves.

"Alright," she said as she squatted down. "Ramona and Daddy, you need to tell me what I should do. Do I stay here, as Mom wants and marry Jeffery, or do I leave and follow my dreams. Do I give up on Jessie coming home?" She stood, anger building. "You two weren't supposed to leave me like this! I've never made a decision in my life without your help. Now what do I do?" she asked. She closed her eyes seeing their smiling faces just like when they would sit on the verandah laughing at her because she always had so much energy.

She could hear her daddy talking. "Charlie, no one can ever tell you what to do, girl. You're too stubborn, I have always believed it's that red hair; you're just like my mother and she was as stubborn as they come." He would lean back in the old rocker on the verandah grinning at her with Ramona laughing and nodding her head in agreement.

Then she saw Ramona grimace and state very plainly, "You would be miserable with Jeffery! He's such a dolt."

"Well, Charlie," she said to herself, "you have your answer. You should decide what to do with your life and no one else."

She walked past the family graves. Her eyes peered down and she read the name. Olivia Rose Bellamead. She looked at a grave next to Olivia's grave. A young boy named Benjamin Randell Bellamead, a Confederate soldier. She gasped. He died when he was sixteen. She had heard the story of Benjamin from her father at night sitting on the verandah. A story passed down from generation to generation.

The story was that in 1863 during the Civil War, Benjamin, the son of William Bellamead, was left to see to the plantation when his father was summoned to a meeting in Charleston to help plan strategies with the news of the Union getting closer. A small militia of Union soldier's had camped down by the river not far from Bella Oak. Late each night, Benjamin would spy on them, as they became the hunted and he the hunter. He would listen and learn about their plans.

One chilly, drizzly night on April twenty-second, Benjamin overheard the Yankee's bragging about an attack that they were planning on Friday, April twenty-fifth, in Charleston. Preparation for the attack was beginning for Brigadier General Quincy Gillmore to lead a large group of Union soldiers into Charleston. The Union soldiers were planning to take the city over but if they couldn't win the battle, then their orders were to burn Charleston. The Yankee's knew the Confederates would be outnumbered because many Confederates had gone north to fight in Virginia.

Benjamin said his goodbyes that morning leaving Bella Oak on his horse named Star Bright. Bravely, he rode that day on a mission to warn the Confederate soldiers who were under the charge of General P.G.T. Beauregard. His efforts that spring day saved many Confederate lives, including his father's life.

He was a true hero with a Confederate victory, but Benjamin Bellamead lost his own life that Friday morning in the battle at Charleston. His lifeless body was placed on his horse and was then covered with a Southern Cross flag. After the battle, his father and a slave named Big John brought the boy home and laid him here to rest in peace."

Charlie reached over and let her fingers gently touch the old stone. "Benjamin Randell Bellamead, the brave young soldier who stands guard over Bella Oak, born December 7th, 1847 died April 25, 1863."

A calming affect came over her. It was a reassurance that he was still here protecting the family plantation. She felt that they were alike in many ways. With the two of them watching over Bella Oak, matters would work out. Her body shivered. She felt someone watching her. She quickly turned around, but didn't see anyone. There on the hill to the side she caught a glimpse of a shadow. She smiled at the shadow, and then she looked down at the grave. She remembered the shadow the day that chased Hudson away, and the same shadow that had hit Jeffery. She whispered, "Benjamin, thank you for watching out for me."

She grabbed hold of Midnight's saddle and leaped upon the chestnut horse. She looked back at the cemetery.

"Good bye, Daddy, Ramona, and Benjamin. I will come back often and visit. I promise to never give up."

Midnight spun around and raced up and down the hills across the pasture and back to the old plantation home.

CHAPTER 24

Always Remember

The Ledford's had given up hope that Jessie was alive and they had moved on with their lives. They planned a memorial service Sunday May the sixth at small church in town.

That sunny Sunday afternoon she entered the church with her mother, Joshua, and Pearl. To the side of the sanctuary was Eli Jones in his clean overalls nervously fidgeting with his hat.

Joshua walked up to him. "Eli, how you doing?"

"Oh, fairly good," Eli answered holding onto his old hat twisting it around and around in a circle. "This ain't easy Joshua. That Jessie was a fine boy and this shouldn't of happened to him. It ain't right."

"I know, but we need to go in and have a seat. Come on and sit with us," Joshua assured, patting the old man on the back.

Eli nodded his head looking over at Charlie. She nodded yes and a smile emerged on his face. He wasn't telling any tales, but you could see he had heard stories about her from Jessie. He turned following Joshua.

The Ledford's sat at the front of the small wooden church and had saved a spot for Charlie to sit next to them. Her body trembled as she made her way to the pew. Her breath was sucked from her lungs. There, in front of her was a picture of Jessie, so realistic she could feel his presence.

The service began as many of the town's folks told stories about Jessie, and even Mr. Kent said a few words about Jessie's great artistic talents and how he was loved by so many. The preacher said a prayer and everyone stood to leave while soft music flowed throughout the church.

Jeffery walked up to Charlie. He softly took hold of her arm pulling her way too close, telling her how sorry he was about Jessie but how glad he was that she and the Ledfords had taken this step of closure. Fire burned in her eyes. Her heart pounded. Her arm jerked away from him and a tight fist grew in her hand. Chandler walked up. He smiled down at her and stepped in between Jeffery and Charlie. Jeffery backed away.

Chandler gently took hold of Charlie's shoulders spinning her around to face him. He whispered in a soft voice. "Now, Charlie, we won't have you punching Jeffery in church, but if anyone needs to punch him, this time it will be me." He stared down on her. "I owe you that."

She reached up to him putting her arms around his large neck. She began to sob as he held onto her. She whispered, "Thank you." Jeffery figured that this was his que to leave, so he turned and walked out of the church.

Chandler leaned over. "Charlie they won't be gone from here as long as we remember them," he said ushering her out of the church and over to Joshua. "I will call you later."

Chandler, she thought, was the one person who understood what she was going through.

She made it home without punching Jeffery. Later that night as she lay in her bed and gazed out her window at the bright stars, she whispered on the spring breeze into the quiet night, "Please, God, send Jessie home to me."

CHAPTER 25

Selling Bella Oak

The school year was coming to an end and Charlie's high school graduation was nearing, but she wasn't celebrating. Too many pieces of her heart lay out in the cemetery. The senior party that she and Ramona had planned didn't exist anymore.

Jeffery never gave up on her; he called day after day and came to visit every chance he got. He would not be deterred on his plan to marry her. The two marrying could blend their plantations and make one of the largest plantations in the South. Jeffery's mother picked out a graduation gift for him to give to Charlie. It was a book about hosting parties, but she could see in his eyes, the gift he wanted to give her was an engagement ring.

Sunday afternoon the thirteenth of May, Charlie sat in the old swing on the veranda looking over the plantation wondering about her future. She leaned back and peered up the ornate columns to the ceiling of the verandah. The front windows framed with black shutters were the eyes of the old plantation, ever watching over the land.

That evening at supper, the night before her graduation from high school, Charlie's mother sat down at the end of the table her face drawn. "Charlene, this is very difficult, but we need to talk." Joshua and Pearl sat quiet their old eyes full of sadness.

"Mom," Charlie questioned as her voice quivered, "is something wrong?"

"This place is too big for us to handle without your father," her mom began. "Joshua can't run it by himself. It's getting too hard on him and I don't have the will or energy to help." Her head turned to Joshua and Pearl. "They have decided to move to North Carolina and lived with their son and grandchildren. I can't run this place on my own and I can't stay here anyway without your father. It's just too depressing," she took in a deep breath. "So – I have decided to sell the plantation."

"Sell Bella Oak!" Charlie screamed jumping from her chair knocking it to the floor. "Mom, I can help run this plantation." Her hands gripped the edge of the table. "Daddy taught me how he and Joshua did everything," Charlie cried out. "You don't have to sell and leave. We will be fine."

"But what about your dreams of moving to Atlanta and not living on this old plantation," Pearl offered. "Honey, Jessie isn't coming back, as much as we all want him to. You know how much I cared for him. Now honey you have to live your life and I'm afraid that staying here is biting off more than you can chew," her head ducked."

"I know Pearl that I have to face the facts about Jessie, but I can't lose Bella Oak too. Please, Mom let me try at least for a while to run the plantation. If it doesn't work, I will give in. I promise," she begged. "Daddy told me right before he died never to give up on anything." She took in a deep breath looking at the three staring at her with their eyes full of tears. They were the only family she had left.

"Well, I don't know Charlie. I can't live here without your father and I am moving to a small home in town. Charlene, I can't stay, and that's that," Martha stoically stated. "You know we haven't made a lot of money the last few years because of all the new agricultural government regulations. I love Bella Oak as much as you do, but it is impractical for you and me to stay here by ourselves. It just won't work."

"Please, Mom, give me a chance to see what I can do. Mr. Ledford will help me, I'm sure, just for a while," she pleaded. "I can pull this off; I know it. I have been helping you with the bills and I understand how to hire the workers for the back fields."

"Charlene, you were planning to leave soon after your graduation. Why would you stay now? Only to help me?" Martha asked looking at her daughter. "Of course, you could marry Jeffery and he would be glad to run this large plantation along with you."

"Oh, Mom, I can't marry Jeffery," Charlie shouted tears welling in her eyes. "I don't know why, but I have to stay. I really can't have you sell Bella Oak without letting me try to run this place and if I have to marry Jeffery to keep it – I will. But, I can't lose this place, too. I have to try and keep it for Daddy."

"Well, if that is what you want, it shouldn't be a problem. Originally, this was going to be all yours someday anyway, but I think you are taking on more than you can handle," Martha said sighing.

"Girl," Joshua said grinning. "If this is what you want." He stood from the table. "I'll help you get started and write down everything you need to do to keep this old plantation going. I believe in you, and you have the gumption to do it. Everett would be proud. I just wished I was twenty years younger and with the two of us we sure would be able to keep Bella Oak the finest plantation in South Carolina, just as she was in her finer days."

Charlie dashed around the table grabbing Joshua. "What am I going to do without the two of you around here?" she asked looking over at Pearl. "You will come back and visit – right?"

"Yes, sweetie, and I will leave you my fried pie recipe so you can learn to make them and keep things going just the same," Pearl said. "I jus' can't stay here. The work is too hard on Joshua and I can't lose him like Everett, way before his time. You know Joshua ain't a spring chicken anymore," she assured smiling at him patting his hand.

"Joshua, before you leave. Please help me finish the first crop in the backfields, and then I can get the cotton planted. I would like to be sure I have all the information that I need and you will only be a phone call away," she declared smiling. "I will keep Bella Oak and make Daddy proud."

Charlie left the room, but she could hear the three talking believing this was a big mistake. She gripped her hands into fist. She'd prove them wrong and she would not have to marry Jeffery if it was the last thing she did. She walked out the back kitchen door and down to the spring.

She sat down on the creek bank in the soft green grass. "Oh, Ramona, this was your dream to live on a plantation, not mine. What have I gotten myself into?" She sat for the next hour watching the fluttering bugs swirling on top of the water.

Charlie walked slowly back to the old house. She had work to do. She hurried into her father's large office. She stopped at the door. She used to come into the office and play while her father worked at his desk. She sat down in the big leather desk chair and her eyes panned the room. Chandler, yes, of course, Chandler! That is who she could ask questions and he wouldn't have any problems helping her with the plantation.

She pulled out her father's journals from the side drawers searching for what needed to be done in the next week. The first crop had been planted and would need to be picked soon. Then she would need to plant the next crop of cotton. She'd learned to drive the tractor almost before she could walk so that wasn't a problem. She knew how to plow the fields that were close to the house and knew how to plant cottonseeds. She sat tallying up how much it cost to plant the crops and hoped she could pull off a good crop of cotton later this summer.

"Hey," Joshua said, coming into the room. "Well Charlie, you shor' look good in that chair." He crossed the room to her. "Those women don't think you can do this, but I have faith in my Charlie. You can work as hard as any boy and shor' are a lot prettier," he said laughing. "I'd be much obliged to help you." He sat down in one of the brown leather chair on the other side of the desk. "Now, let me show you a few tricks and every time I think of something, I will jot it down for you."

She smiled staring up at the old face and she could see that his heart was breaking along with hers to think about leaving. This was his home, where he was born. "Thank you, Joshua."

"We ain't leaving for a couple of weeks, so I can help you start bringing in the first crop. That will help your bottom line. This year ain't going to be as hard as the last few years. We sold the cattle off the first of the year so you don't have to worry about them until next year," he laughed. "The chickens, you have been taken care of them since you were their size. I have decided to leave Betsy here; she's a good guard dog and can help you keep the snakes out of the spring, that is if you want her."

"That would be great. She belongs here anyway. Joshua, I have to pull this off, I can't lose Bella Oak."

"God isn't going to give up on you, girl – you'll be triumphant," he said nodding his head yes, wiping his eyes standing to leave.

The next week Charlie busily helped her mom move into town and helped Joshua and Pearl pack their things. The house was becoming empty with boxes sitting everywhere.

Joshua would sit until late at night and help show her how the business of the plantation worked. She was catching on, believing more and more she could do this work; she was confident.

The day arrived to say goodbye to Joshua and Pearl. Martha and Charlie stood on the verandah. She couldn't breathe; this couldn't be real, losing Joshua and Pearl.

Everyone hugged. Pearl stood on the steps and Joshua took her arm and led her to the old pickup. He closed the driver side door and the truck turned around and drove down the tree-lined path and turned onto the dirt road disappearing just as Jessie did that day almost a year ago.

"Well, Charlene, I need to be going to town," Martha said. "I have a lot of unpacking to do. Honey, call me if you need anything," Martha gripped her tight. "I'm still uneasy about leaving you out here all alone.

"I'm fine, Mom," Charlie admitted. "The Ledford's are right here, and I have ole Betsy and my peashooter."

"Okay," Martha called back, walking down the steps. She sat in her car for a few minutes staring at the old plantation home. "I mean it, call me, Charlene, if you need anything," she called out driving down the path to the gate.

"Well, Charlie, this is your new life," she said to herself. The first thing was to go to her bedroom. There she methodically chose a few of Jessie's drawings. Carefully holding onto them she made her way downstairs to the living room. Her mom had taken pictures off the walls to use in her new home and Charlie wanted to replace them with Jessie's drawings.

"There, that's better," she said standing with her hands on her hips studying the pictures of her past. The sketches of her and Ramona and their life down at the spring suited her. "Now…one more for the office, the one of Joshua and Daddy." She placed it on the wall right in front of her desk. "Now, it's really my home." She slapped her hands together. "Okay Charlie, this isn't going to be so bad," she said making her way to the kitchen.

She picked up the list that Joshua had helped her with containing the chores for each day. She tugged her boots on along with her straw hat. She walked past the long rows of small-deteriorated brick outhouses that were sitting out to the far back of the plantation home that once were used for slaves. She'd heard the stories that many of the freed slaves after the Civil War stayed on the plantation and worked not ever leaving. If her grandfathers of the past were like her father, she could easily understand the reason for some of the slaves staying. This was their home.

She finished the list for the day. She walked up to the back of the house exhausted. She smiled, it felt good, and she had made it on her own for one day.

She stepped over Betsy and opened the kitchen screen door, but stopped. She leaned down and patted Betsy's head. Her boots slid off and she hung her hat on the hook in the laundry room and stepped slowly up the stairs to the bathroom.

Her exhausted body slid deep into the tub. The warm water felt so relaxing and she ducked her head under swishing it back and forth so she could wash her hair. Oh, this felt good to her weary body. She lay in the warm water dreaming of what her life should've been. The water began to cool so she stepped out of the tub reaching for a towel to dry her long hair. She dried her hair as much as she could with the towel, but the rest would have to air dry. Her eyes caught a glimpse of her reflection in the mirror, a tired, lonely girl. She could almost cry. She grabbed a pair of jean shorts out of the dresser drawer. Lying next to them was her tie-dyed shirt from last summer, making her thoughts go back to a better time at Bella Oak.

She stared in the mirror at her wild hair, amused. She could hear Ramona laughing. "Charlie you have the wildest red hair in the county." Ramona would then try and help her brush out the tangled mess but it never did any good.

She laid the hairbrush on the dresser and wiped the tears from her eyes. Was this going to be her new life, talking to herself? The bedroom light clicked off leaving shadows in the room. She stepped out into the long hallway making her way downstairs to the kitchen. She slowed her pace on the staircase listening to the moaning of each step. The noise was a familiarity of each board's sound by heart. Tiredness was overcoming her, but Pearl had left plenty of food so she wouldn't go hungry for a while. Pearl had frozen some meals so Charlie just had to warm them in the oven.

She leaned back in the tall-backed kitchen chair taking a bite of meatloaf. The calm night was filled with the language of katydids, frogs, and crickets. It was a peaceful evening as she sat at the kitchen table and stared out the window seeing the bright moon shining down through the tall trees. She finished cleaning the last glass in the sudsy sink's water letting the dishes drain in the drain board. The dishtowel hung on the handle of the oven to dry. She latched the hook on the kitchen screen door to lock it, and then she closed the kitchen wooden door; there she was done for the night.

The front door screen screaked as she pushed it open. She stepped out onto the verandah and made her way over to the swing. The swing slowly swung back and forth. Times of the past flowed in her head. Her eyes closed. Voices of her father, mother, Jessie, Ramona, and so many people murmured along with laughter filled her mind.

"Thump!" Charlie's eyes sprung open. She jumped from the swing and grabbed her peashooter. Her heart pounded. She let out a breath of air and sighed.

"Oh…it's you girl." She stared down at Betsy. The old dog came near and Charlie leaned over petting the hound dog as she placed her pistol back into its holster. "Now, Charlie you have to get used to this abundance of quiet," she assured herself.

She peered down at Betsy. "You already miss everyone too. It is too quiet. Come on and sit by me. At least I won't be talking to myself."

She laughed. The dog circled a few times, wiggled, and lay down by the steps. Her sad eyes peered up at Charlie.

Days and nights moved on. This was Charlie's new life, day after day. Occasionally on Sunday afternoons after church, she and Betsey would sneak down to the spring and swim. It was a way to cope and clear her mind. Plus, Charlie could talk to Ramona just as she always did.

One hot sultry evening, Charlie sat in the swing on the veranda relaxing. She heard a car motor, she jumped from the swing. Her body sighed. It was too late to run and hide seeing the blue convertible thunderbird pulling into the drive.

"Oh, Mom, why did you tell Jeffery I was here alone?" she wondered as she took in a deep breath watching as the car pulled to a stop.

Jeffery opened the car door a huge grin emerged on his face. "Good evening, Charlie. How are things going," he asked, stepping up onto the verandah.

Betsy growled and Charlie laughed. Jeffery crossed the verandah and sat down in the swing next to her letting his very expensive boots gently push the swing back and forth.

"I saw your mom in town yesterday. She said you are staying on the plantation and running it. That is some undertaking, my lady. I know if anyone can do it, though, you can." He stopped the swing, turned his head to her, and stared her in the eyes. "I thought you were leaving for the big city after your graduation?"

"I was, but my plans have changed and now I am staying here. Don't look at me as if I'm crazy. Things are going just fine," she said. She scooted away from him to the side of the swing. She saw his smile grow on his face. This was his dream for her to stay on this plantation, marry him, and live right here. It was all coming true, he thought.

"Isn't it lonely sitting here in this big house all by yourself?"

"No, I have Betsy."

"You know what I mean. Don't you miss talking to someone."

"I'm really doing fine, Jeffery."

"Well…I'm home for the summer, so if you need any help just call. I do know more about working a plantation than I did last year. I do know, without a doubt, it's a lot of work for my father and he has two foremen to help."

"I'm not working the whole plantation, just half to begin with. That's enough to keep things going."

"You wouldn't happen to have some whisky would you? It has been a long day," he asked, leaning back in the swing getting comfortable.

She took a deep breath; he wasn't going to leave soon. "Sure, come on in." She pulled the door open and he followed close behind her. She showed him her father's liquor cabinet in the dining room. She wasn't going to stop in the living room and let him see Jessie's drawings. He made himself at home pouring a tumbler of whisky. He stood proud, taking in the room, ready to be the owner and proprietor of this fine plantation. His eyes landed on her father's captain's chair at the head of the dining room table. She could see the wheels turning. Jeffery was an easy read, and his face revealed that he was ready to assume the head of the household.

She quickly suggested that they go back outside on the verandah. The cool night air was refreshing as they sat in the swing. Charlie looked over at him sitting so smug holding his drink in his hand. He slowly moved the swing back and forth trying to carry on a normal conversation. He did know most of the gossip in town and what everyone from school was doing. He bragged about his school trying to impress Charlie. He was going one more year to school, which was enough to get an associate degree in agriculture, and then would be coming back to run the Montgomery Plantation. She knew he had his plans which included his willingness to run this plantation as well.

"Jeffery, it's getting late and I have to get up early in the morning."

"I'm sure you do." He leaned near, "I hate to see you working so hard with those pretty little hands." His head shook feeling the beginning of calluses. "You shouldn't be out doing manual labor. I can hire a few men to come over and help you out for a while," he said tenderly as his fingers pushed her wild red hair from her face.

"That's very nice," she said jumping from the swing to get away from him. He stood from the swing and looked down on her as if to say, "It's just a matter of time." Jeffery was very handsome with his long, curly, brown hair, hazel eyes, and broad shoulders. Many women in the county would be glad to marry him.

She walked over to the steps, "I don't need any help. I am handling things, Jeffery. I want to do this. Thank you anyway."

"I'm just a phone call away and I will be checking on you," he said getting way to close again, pulling her next to him. "I don't like you living out here all alone. Once everyone knows you're out here by yourself, you could become a target. It's just plain dangerous for a beauty like you to by yourself and work yourself to death. "

She could see that he believed, like so many others, that she didn't have a snowball's chance in hell making this work. He figured that she would be calling him soon, begging him for help.

"You know…." He said softly moving her hair from her face, looking into those green eyes. "I could come out each day and help you run the old plantation so you wouldn't be alone. You know with my help, life would be a lot easier on you. Charlie, we don't have to beat around the bush anymore, you know how I feel about you."

"I have Betsy and I never go anywhere without my pistol. I can take care of myself. I also have the Ledfords. They are right over there."

"Oh, I forgot about those people," he said irritably. "Too bad you can't buy them out and make them move." He smirked. "They'd be better off."

"They are my friends," she squinted. Her face heated with anger. Still the same ol' Jeffery, a snobbish fool. He leaned down to kiss her but she turned her head, his kiss landed on her cheek. "Good night, Jeffery."

"Good night," Jeffery stepped down from the verandah. He strutted to his car full of confidence. "Call me if you need anything," he yelled slowly driving off.

She knew it would be a cold day in hell before she called him for help. Watching his tail lights disappear into the night, was a welcomed sight.

The next couple of weeks Jeffery stopped by a few times and she got rid of him as fast as she could. Time was moving on, it was now the end of June, and the first crop was finally in. She paid the hired workers and set up for them to come back later on in the summer to pick the cotton.

Next, the second crop needed to be planted. The field hands had planted the cotton crop out from the house, but she was planning on working the field that her father always planted to save some money. She had to prove she could run this plantation. Each day was tiring and wearing on her, but she wasn't going to let her mom or Jeffery know.

That evening, she pushed the swing gradually back and forth while tears ran down her face. This was harder than she had ever imagined, loneliness was overwhelming, and she felt so empty inside. She couldn't lose the plantation and she just couldn't marry Jeffery. She always kept her gun close, never letting her guard down. Her eyes panned the yard into the dark night. She leaned back in the swing her mind drifted off into a deep sleep.

•••

She shivered. Her eyes blinked, in front of her were the blue eyes she had fallen in love with. His hand reached out to her. She placed her hand in his as he pulled her up next to him. His gentle fingers pushed her long red hair from her face. Softly, he lifted her face up to him. She passionately held him close feeling his heartbeat, her body giving in. Her body shook when the swing moved. Her head ducked.

"No," she whispered, "please don't leave." For a fleeting second, she felt his tender touch and then – he was gone. This was her dream many nights and it ended the same way. Her body was left feeling warm from the love and passion she had missed.

She leaned against the back of the swing; the stabbing in her chest was intense. Her dream of Jessie returning had faded, but not her memories. She'd always cherish the time they spent together. Her daddy had told her she was lucky, many people live a lifetime and never feel the love she'd felt.

She sucked in the night air. She squeezed her hands into fist as she swung them in the air. "Daddy, I will make it, I promise. I will get the next crop planted and make enough money to run the plantation at least for another year. I will show everyone and you will be proud."

Tears began to slide down her face.

"Jessie, I will always love you."

CHAPTER 26

Hidden Dreams

Monday morning came early; it was the twenty-fifth of June. The realization was difficult for Charlie. There wouldn't be a Bella Oak Fourth of July party this year. There wasn't any way for her to work the plantation and have a party too.

That morning, Charlie was up before the sun, knowing the temperature was going to get unseasonably hot that afternoon. She grabbed a bowl from the cabinet to make herself some breakfast, another bowl of cereal, not a breakfast Pearl would have made. Her eyes moved to the kitchen screen door. She stared outside. She shuddered. The warm morning sun was already beginning to shine.

She sat a pitcher of ice water and a cup on the front porch making her way to the barn. It was going to be a long hot day. The tractor's motor started. She sighed relief. Her hand patted the tractor as if it were alive, saying thank you. She smelled the scent of tractor fuel and warm pine needles telling her summer had arrived. Only a whisper of a breeze was blowing through the top of the tall pines.

The heat from the scorching sun blared down on her. She wiped the sweat from her face. Time was speeding by at a fast pace, but she wasn't wavering to finish planting the field today, stopping for only a quick lunch. She continued throughout the afternoon plowing the huge field until the day finally ended as the sun began to sink in the sky. Tomorrow she'd plant the cottonseeds and then she would be able to rest.

Once more, she didn't want to leave the warm bath water. Her long hair floated in the water as she talked to herself. Reluctantly, she dressed and went downstairs. She had left the pantry door open. Looking inside, she whispered, "Thank you, Pearl." There were still a few jars of blackberry jam. Yet another supper of peanut butter and jam sandwich.

That evening was like the rest. She lifted an old record from the table in the living room and caressed it to her chest. She carefully laid the record on the turntable and gently set the needle arm down. Her body tingled to listen to her and Jessie's song, *Will You Still Love Me Tomorrow*. The words flowed out the open living room window onto the verandah. She sat down in the swing and gently pushed it with her toes to the rhythm of the song, quietly singing along. Charlie's eyes closed and a movie of Jessie and Ramona played clearly in her mind about that night when they sat in her room and sang along with the recording.

A couple of hours went by as Charlie rocked herself in the swing. Betsy always lay at the top of the steps. Charlie smiled and talked to her. Time was helping and she was getting used to her life on the plantation.

The next morning came too soon. She struggled to sit up in her bed. She looked down at Betsy her only companion. "Oh, Betsy," she moaned, "I don't know if I can pull this off." The hound dog's ears perked up listening to her talk. Charlie's eyes swung to the mirror over her dresser.

She flipped the bed covers to the side, climbed out of bed, and moved to the mirror. "Now Charlie," she said giving a strong stare, "you can't let your Daddy down or give in to Jeffery." She stomped her foot.

The morning was the same. The empty bowl of cereal was placed in the sink and the pitcher of water was set on the porch. The hot sun was blaring down, but Charlie wasn't giving up. The seeds had to be planted. This was her only chance to save the plantation and she wasn't going to quit.

The day wore on. She wiped the sweat from her brow and swished her wet ponytail releasing it from the back of her neck. "Yes," she yelled, spinning around watching the sun quickly sink in the sky. "I did it!" she yelled, again. "I am going to make it. I did it. I got the field planted." She limped as she walked to the house but a huge smile was on her face as she made her way up the stairs to the bathroom.

Her dirty smelly clothes slowly dropped to the floor. She stared in the mirror at the dirt-streaked face with dark circles showing under her puffy eyes. Her head shook; that couldn't be her. Again, her body slipped into the warm soothing bath water letting the water cuddled her aching body. Her hair swished softly flowing from side to side as she rinsed out the shampoo and then she leaned back. Her eyes closed. Oh, she flinched opening her eyes. She didn't want to fall asleep but she didn't want to move. Unwillingly, she climbed out of the old claw-footed tub. She stood still for a few seconds staring into the mirror seeing her thin body.

She slid the comb through her wet, tangled hair. She had figured out that if she didn't try to towel dry it, her hair would not get so tangled. She let it fall down her back drying naturally. She didn't have anyone to impress. She laughed at her freckles across her nose popping out from being outside all day in the hot sun. With her jean shorts and t-shirt slipped on, she stopped to look at Jessie's drawing of her last year. Her body shivered. Had it only been a year since he left for the Army? It seemed more of an eternity in her mind. She softly whispered to herself, "Charlie, you can make it now. You must."

She believed that she and the plantation were going to survive. But, she felt like her heart was becoming callused, now just as her hands. If that was what it was going to take to survive, then so be it. She was a survivor just as her father had said and she had to believe life would become easier, as time moved on.

She stepped slowly down the stairs every muscle in her body ached. She stopped by the front door listening to the creaking, and moaning of the old home cooling off from the summer sun's heat. The old plantation home had made it through tough times and so would she.

Charlie walked through the parlor turned on the lamp that sat in the corner by her daddy's chair, the one he sat in every night, a routine she practiced each night so she didn't feel so alone. Her eyes closed seeing her daddy sitting in the chair reading a book. She headed to the kitchen, made herself another peanut butter and jam sandwich and tried to eat but she was too exhausted. She sat at the table making a vow that next week she'd cook herself some nice meal, since all the food that Pearl had left in the freezer was gone.

A clap of thunder shook the house. "No," she yelled, dropping her sandwich on her plate. The screen down flew open as she ran outside on the verandah. The wind swirled blowing the old oaks. The dark clouds rolled in, droplets of rain began to fall, and the thunder continued to shake the house.

"Please God, give the seeds a few days," she begged staring up into the darkening sky. The raindrops grew larger pounding the hard ground. Now the rain was coming down in bucketful after bucketful. Streams of water rushed across the hard dry ground and poured into the low places. It was a flash flood!

Charlie's body slid down to the floor of the veranda. She leaned against the house, her knees pulled to her chest. She sobbed with her head in her hands. "Why, God? I've tried so hard!" she cried out as an avalanche of tears flowed down her face.

Betsy nuzzled against her. Thirty minutes later the rain slowed and the thunder and lightning moved on. She pushed her sore body from the verandah floor, darted down the steps, and ran out to the field. The last of the rain drops soaked her. She slid to a complete stop.

The field was covered in water. It looked like a lake instead of a field, a total loss! Both days of work were gone. She'd have to plow and seed the field again. The seeds she'd just planted had floated away. This thunderstorm had a vengeance, just as Hurricane Cleo had, sending down inches of rain in a short period of time.

Her body trembled in the dark night. Her head leaned back watching the black clouds floating away and the moon lighting up the night. She didn't move feeling her long hair dripping cold water down her back.

Someone grabbed her.

Charlie screamed and thought; it's Jeffery. "Stop, stop it!" she yelled, spun around, and hit him on the chest with both fists.

"Red – it's me,"

Standing in front of her was the love of her life. Nobody else called her *Red*. Had she died out in the field like her daddy? Was this just a dream?

She felt his hands wrap around her pulling her near. Gently, he pushed her wet hair from her face. He softly lifted her face up to him.

"Jessie, how!" she screamed.

"I was shot in the shoulder and held prisoner for months in Vietnam. All I could think about was you. Thoughts of you kept me from losing my mind. I prayed every day to be rescued. Finally, our guys liberated the camp where I was, and the rest is history. It took me a while to recover, but I'm back and I'm never leaving you again," he said. He leaned down kissing her in the moonlight.

"Poppa told me what you are doing, Red, and why you're doing it. Red, I'm sorry about your dad. He was the best man I ever knew, outside of my own dad."

"Daddy told me never to give up on you, that you would come home to me. Oh, Jessie, I don't care about my dreams of Atlanta anymore or about losing this crop. I never gave up hope that you'd come home," she said softly. She could hear his heart beating as he held her close. She wanted to believe he was real and not her imagination or another dream.

"Come on, let's get inside. I don't want you to get sick," he whispered softly.

There standing on the top step wiggling her tail was Betsy. "Hey, Betsy old girl," Jessie said leaning down rubbing her ears. "How ya doing girl, I missed you too," he said as she turned over for him to scratch her belly.

Jessie opened the screen door and stepped inside the living room. He stopped and smiled seeing all of his drawings hanging on the walls.

"That was the way I kept you alive," Charlie said, "but now you can draw me new ones." She closed and opened her eyes wondering. Was this a dream? She looked up. Jesse was real and he hadn't disappeared. "This is our home now, Jessie, if you would like." Tears of joy flowed down her face.

He kissed her, giving her his answer.

She touched his face feeling the scar from the hurricane. Yes, it was really Jessie. "We need to get some dry clothes on. I still have some of Daddy's clothes upstairs." She grabbed his arm leading him up the stairs.

Jessie put on some of Everett's clothes. They were a few sizes too big, but they were dry. She stood in the bathroom drying off. Charlie looked in the mirror at her swollen red eyes and wild hair. "Gee, I'm a real mess," she sighed. She wrapped her hair with a towel and put a cool wet cloth on her eyes. She looked at her wild hair drying. She laughed it would dry like the red fox's tail Jessie told her about, the day when they were sitting in the old oak tree. Charlie slipped on some shorts and a t-shirt and raced downstairs.

She kept saying over and over in her mind, "This is real and not a dream."

She stopped at the bottom of the stairs. Jessie stood quietly staring at his drawings. She didn't move for a minute, studying him. He was thinner like her, but taller with shorter blonde hair.

He moved to the record player and placed the needle arm gently on the record. The music rang out into the room and he softly sang the chorus, "Will you still love me tomorrow," just as he had done that night in her room.

She quietly walked to him. Her arms tenderly wrapped around him as she sang her answer, "Yes, I will love you tomorrow and always."

"I have dreamed of this for the last year, holding you, kissing you, loving you."

"This is real, isn't it, Jessie? You're really here?" she asked.

"Yes, I'm really here, holding you, and I'm not ever leaving. I promise… Now – Miss Charlene "Charlie" Olivia Bellamead," he announced getting down on one knee, "Red, will you marry me, a poor boy from across the spring. I have nothing to give you, except my love and my drawings.

"Yes, Mr. Jessie Lee Ledford," she answered softly saying the words she had only dream of saying. "Only if you will give up that stubborn pride, live here at Bella Oak, and take this plantation as your own. Oh, this would be a proud day for Daddy. He loved you and he'd be so excited for us."

"Ramona would feel the same way. She'd be jumping with joy."

He kissed her again. The night became more wonderful than either could have imagined and they both understood this was only the beginning of their lives together. They caressed each other with passion bringing back memories of that beautiful day down by the spring, letting the lone lamp gave off a soft glow as they stared into each other eyes.

Charlie's sore muscles relaxed with his tender touch. Her heart fluttered with warm emotions. As their bodies embraced, they engulfed each other.

A loud clap of thunder and a bright lightning bolt lit the room neither noticed the thunderstorm moving in, their thoughts only on each other not worried about anything.

The next evening, the blue convertible drove down the drive. Jeffery once more showed up to check on Charlie unannounced. The car pulled to a stop and he stepped out of his car. His body slumped staring at the veranda.

Jessie sat on the swing next to Charlie his arm around her.

Jessie stood from the swing. "Hi, Jeffery! How are you? Charlie told me you'd been checking on her since you got home from college. I can't tell you how much that means to both of us," Jessie reached out his hand. Jeffery was absolutely dumbfounded for a moment but finally shook his head and extended his hand too.

Bella Oak did have its Fourth of July party that year, just as normal with a little twist of hidden dreams, a wedding.

The long, white silk gown of Grandmother Charlene's swirled in a circle; the same wedding gown Charlie's mother had worn when she married Everett.

Charlie grabbed hold of Chandler by the shoulders. "Ramona would be happy for Jessie and me today. She also wouldn't want you to be alone, Chandler. She wouldn't." Charlie fought back tears, "No, I'm not crying today. It's the happiest day of my life, and I'm not going to cry because Ramona wouldn't want me to."

"Charlie," Chandler said, "You're right. This was Ramona's dream, you know, for you and Jessie to marry and live here on Bella Oak. She had big plans for the four of us. She could smile and make the world right."

"Yes, I can see her in my mind standing to the side with a big smile on her face," Charlie replied.

"Thank you, Charlie I needed to hear that it is alright for me to move on and to find someone else to love. You know – it has been hard on me to go on with my life," he sniffed. "I miss Ramona so much, and I will always love her."

"I understand, but Leann is right for you. Ramona loved you so much, and I know that she's smiling on us from Heaven, wanting us to gather up as much happiness as we possibly can. We both are going to make it now."

Chandler grinned, "Well, at this moment, we have a wedding to get started, and we sure don't want to keep Jessie waiting. He has waited long enough." He tenderly slid her arm in his as they crossed the living room to the screen door making their way down the old path to the creek.

This Fourth of July wedding was perfect standing by the cool stream. Even with the bright sun shining down, the old live oaks shaded the wedding setting. Beams of sunlight occasionally touched the faces of Jessie and Charlie. Charlie could feel Ramona and her daddy near.

Jessie stood tall. He winked telling Charlie everything was all right. *Someday* had arrived and their hidden dream was now reality.

Chandler put his arm around Leann. He looked over at Charlie with a big smile on his face. Carol and Billy Mac were happily waiting for this November when a new little Tolleson would be born. Everyone was there, including Jeffery and Vanessa. Vanessa was over the top to finally be with Jeffery.

Martha gave in accepting that Jessie was perfect for Charlie. Pearl was beside herself when she heard the news and said they'd visit in October, so she could help Charlie learn to make fried apple pies. She couldn't let the biggest fan of her fried pies go without for very long.

Jessie took charge of the plantation with his father's help. His parents moved into Joshua and Pearl's home. Life was wonderful for Jessie and Charlie, but they did as they promised and never forgot Ramona or the good times they had when they were young.

Joshua and Pearl would visit each summer for years on the Fourth of July, and Joshua would sit on the veranda talking about the old plantation watching it grow into the most prosperous plantation in the South. Joshua and Charlie knew Everett was proud looking down on his beloved plantation and seeing Jessie manage it so well.

Jessie placed a bench on the bank by the spring creek and he and Charlie would sit for hours in the evenings talking, while he would sit and draw. He finally let others see his drawings and the Associated Press featured him in a two-page spread in newspapers across the country. Eventually, Jessie's art was featured at Bachman Crane Gallery in New York City. Corporate and private collectors throughout the world relied on Bachman Crane to locate and acquire exemplary works of art for them. Jessie started out as a noteworthy artist, but in time, he was recognized for his masterworks and became wealthy on his own. The best of his drawings were of Charlie and Ramona at the spring creek. Those he would never part with.

Each Fourth of July Charlie and Jessie would celebrate their anniversary sitting watching their own children, Everett, Julia, and one redhead named Ramona. They would play in the spring with all of the other children from the area, making dreams of their own. Chandler and Leann would bring their five children, and they would tell about when they were young and the times they would swim in the spring-fed creek.

Charlie and Jessie did as they promised and never forgot the times they spent down at the spring with Ramona. Hidden dreams had been twisted together to bond their lives forever.

Charlie added to her journal from her childhood and of times in the distant past. She wanted her children and each generation to learn of the story of a beautiful girl, their aunt named Ramona and a kind man, their grandfather, Everett, who would have loved them so. She kept the journal along with the Jessie's drawings telling a simple story of how to never give up on love or life. Always believe in yourself, just as her father told her.

Jessie and Charlie did travel the world and they were able to see many cities, including Paris and Rome, but they were always happy to return to Bella Oak. Charlie knew that she'd stay there the rest of her life, just as her ancestors before her, and she'd sit in the old swing on the veranda to watch their children and then, their grandchildren: Benjamin, Kevin, and Candace. She believed one of the children would love Bella Oak as she did and would decide to live at the plantation one day.

Charlie and Jessie sat year after year on their bench by the spring as time moved on. They watched the cool water softly trickle over the dam they'd built so long ago remembering their Southern dreams of yesterday and living on the plantation that captured their hearts.

Jessie leaned over pulling Charlie close, and she looked into those blue eyes that she adored.

"Well, Red – the tears of sorrow have vanished into the stream and the tears of joy have appeared." He grinned sitting on their bench finishing the last bite of his fresh fried apple pie.

About the Author

Diann Shaddox is a Native American Indian and a member of the Wyandotte Nation of Oklahoma and she has Essential Tremors. She's an award-winning author of *A Faded Cottage, Whispering Fog, Miranda, Spirits of Sacred Mountain, The Gatekeeper,* and *Southern Dreams* Series.

Diann is the Founder of Diann Shaddox Foundation, a Non-Profit 501c(3) public organization fighting the battle to find a cure and bring awareness for Essential Tremor, (ET).

Diann was born on December 18th in a small southern town of Nashville, Arkansas, the youngest and only daughter of William and Mary Ann Shaddox. But, fate stepped in and William, a crop-duster, at the age of 25, died in a plane crash on November 20th, a month before she was born, therefore, Diann was never able to meet her father. Mary Ann, who grew up in Miami, Oklahoma, moved back to Miami after William's death, where Diann lived until her mother died when she was only 3 years old. Diann then moved to Nashville, Arkansas to live with her grandparents. At the age of 10, Diann's Granddad Holt died of a stroke, leaving her grandmother alone to see to her.

Diann learned from an early age about death and how life should not be squandered. Her Mamow Holt, who had lost her right hand in an accident at a factory in Nashville, Arkansas, taught her, you never give up. Her grandmother never let anything stand in her way. She taught herself to write, cook, and even how to sew and make quilts with her left hand, without any prosthetics. Being handicapped was a word she never used.

Growing up in a small town was wonderful, learning to fish, growing a garden and the most important thing, patience of a grandmother. Stories from the past evolved of family bringing many stories to life. Sitting out late at night on cool summer evenings, swinging on an old swing staring up at the stars helped Diann's vivid imagination grow.

On May 20, 2014, Diann's son Rick died of a brain tumor.

She has an enthusiasm for travel and living life to its fullest. You have only one life and shouldn't waste it. The zest for meeting and getting to know people is a very important component in her life. She is a believer of herbs, natural and organic foods, and a big supporter of Bio-identical Hormones and keeping our planet green.

Diann has resided in eight great states, Arkansas, Oklahoma, Kentucky, New Jersey, Virginia, Texas, Florida, and now South Carolina.

www.diannshaddox.com

Diann Shaddox Foundation for Essential Tremor

The Diann Shaddox Foundation for Essential Tremor is a Non-Profit 501 c(3) public organization dedicated to finding a cure for Essential tremor, educate, and increase awareness about people afflicted with Essential Tremors, the largest and most common movement disorder in the world.

We at DSF believe we can make a difference in millions of people's lives and directly change the future for everyone who will inherit or develop Essential Tremors. We want to show that Essential Tremor isn't just for the elderly, but children of all ages have ET. Most people though haven't heard about Essential Tremor and Diann Shaddox Foundation for Essential Tremor is adamant to bring attention to the world.

Essential Tremor (ET) is a progressive neurological condition that causes a rhythmic trembling of the hands, head, voice, legs, or body. ET can begin at any age, from birth to 100 and doesn't discriminate with age, race, sex, or national origin. Over 42 million people worldwide have Essential Tremor. Recent research indicates that 5 out of every 100 children under the age of 20 has Essential Tremor.

To learn more, go to www.diannshaddoxfoundation.org

DIANN SHADDOX

HISTORY OF CROSSWAYS, AIKEN, SC THE PLANTATION HOME ON ALL SOUTHERN DREAMS BOOK COVER

Distinctly Southern and an integral part of Aiken's history, Crossways was built before the incorporation of Aiken, before the Hitchcock's and the Winter Colony put Aiken on the map, and before John Gary Evans belted out his acceptance speech for the nomination to the office of governor from the second story balcony.

Circa 1815, Crossways was built by the burgeoning cotton industry that flourished before the Civil War. The home was the centerpiece of a 368 acre cotton plantation in what was then the Barnwell District. Though little is known about the property prior to the Civil War, in 1868 it was purchased by James L Derby, a New York publisher and partner in the Aiken Land Improvement Company. Derby moved his family to Aiken in 1868. The property at that point had been sold down to 25 acres and was often referred to as Derby Farm or Derby Mansion.

The Derby Mansion with 25 acres was sold to Henry Watkins in 1872. The Watkins owned the property until 1875, when they sold the home and 25 acres to Edward Henry.

Henry was from Boston, but he was a Southern sympathizer and had settled for a time in Charleston. Here he met his future wife, Harriet Lythgoe, and became a shipbuilder and blockade runner.

For several years the home was occupied, but not owned by John Gary Evans. Evans served in the SC House and Senate and was elected Governor in 1894.

In 1899 the home and 30 acres was acquired from the estate of Mrs. Henry by a prominent Aiken dentist, H.G. Ray for $5,500. The family of George Monroe was known to have lived in the home in the early

1900's. It seems the name "Crossways" came into being about this time. It has been suggested to stem from the irregular, crossways setting of the home on the property.

Ray sold the property in 1927 for $40,000 to Arthur Young, an accountant and business man. Arthur Young founded Arthur Young & Company, an international accounting firm which ultimately has become part of the Ernest & Young firm. Young spent another $35,000 doing major additions and changes to the home as reported in local news of 1927. Young died in 1948 after which the property was sold to P.J. Boatwright, a cotton merchant.

The Boatwright's desired to have their four children nearby and deeded lots facing Banks Mill Road to each; shrinking the property to 2 acres as the housing boom demanded land for families coming to Aiken. In 1954, Mr. & Mrs. Harold Sanders from Dallas, Texas came to Aiken with the Savannah River Plant and acquired the home.

In 1987 the home was sold to Canadians, William & Leslie Stirling as a winter residence. Mr. Stirling took the task of documenting the house's history and significance and got it placed on the National Registry of Historic Places in 1996.

In 1998 Wisconsin transplants, Patrick & Gail Pratt purchased the property.

In 2007, Bob & Jane Hottensen, also from Wisconsin purchased the property as a winter retreat.

With continued respect to Crossways, the Hottensen's undertook the most ambitious recent renovations, including annexation of several residential lots around Crossways. Their efforts have integrated the home into a much larger presentation – fitting of its name – Crossways Plantation.

Over 200 years old now, Crossways represents the grace, ease, and elegance of a time past.

www.ingramcontent.com/pod-product-compliance
Lightning Source LLC
Chambersburg PA
CBHW021656110726
47902CB00007B/1957